I0683052

THE PARALLEL LINE

The Steve Kaufman Series #2

Elliot Lei

West Ridge Publishing Co.

For Rhonda, a/k/a Becky Dean.

CHAPTER ONE

Steve Kaufman buried his head in his hands, kneeling against the commode on the bathroom of her hospital room, then staring at the faded, green-flecked linoleum floor, begging the Almighty for life, his wife of only two years lying with tubes and bandages on a bed meant for the sick and dying.

He was familiar with the concept of the dying having their lives flashback before their final moments, but now, oddly, he found his own thoughts doing the same. The time he lost his first love, Lily, in the summer of 68' just days before the Democratic National Convention, then to his college graduation in 71' when he would see his grandmother for the last times that summer staying with Uncle Marv and Aunt Denise in Scottsdale, working in his office for him as a real estate assistant and how he never kept the air conditioning on for very long.

His thoughts returned to Lily. The last time he saw her, they were making love in her basement, a time he will never forget, where they made plans for the rest of their lives. And then she was gone, killed by a hit-and-run driver. Oh my gosh, he thought. Look at what happens with me and serious relationships. Women end up dead.

A rumbling noise startled him from the hall, like a bed or big cart being wheeled towards the room, as it seemed to get louder. But then it went past, thank goodness, and he returned to his thoughts. Now he was back in 1972 when he started school for his Master of Management degree at Northwestern. He had long been interested in business, much to his father's chagrin, who wanted him to follow in his own footsteps as a physician. He knew that since he made that life decision, despite his father's supposed support, there was a feeling of resentment that the son had almost chosen an opposite career path on purpose just for spite.

Then it was 1974, he was at the restaurant on Belmont Avenue where he ran into Sam Kupfer, a patient of his father's, who was having lunch with Alvin Ryerson, who ran Ryerson Savings and Loan. When he told him he had just graduated from school with a business/management degree, he ended up starting at the bank a week later as a junior loan officer with two guys in their sixties ahead of him in a three-man operation.

He smiled for a second as he remembered the elderly tellers and customers who had been with the bank long before he was born. Two years later, they made him a second vice president even though he had closed maybe a dozen loans. He was twenty-six, the youngest V.P. the bank ever had. He lived in a nice apartment in Sandburg Village with a roommate from grad school, had a handful of friends, mostly from college, dated but never anything serious, and by 1981 was a full V.P. with an office next to Sam Ryerson's.

But he was bored. He knew other bankers and people in management who were leading more exciting lives, at least in business. The loan limit at Ryerson's for everything, commercial, industrial, vacant land for investment, etc., was set at six million. Even Mr. Ryerson stuck to that. Through the years, many deals had to be passed up because of it. It was archaic in the overall banking world, but the bank board, which was basically Sam Ryerson and his brother Al, would never bend. It was clearly limiting his own future as well as his well-being.

Going on seven damned years.

Meanwhile, in that January of 80' he met someone he thought was the one. And she was. It was on a Saturday evening at a downtown hotel just off Michigan Avenue. A University of Illinois Alumni Association function. There was a small cash bar inside, but it was also oppressively hot there. By nine, many people were gravitating outside to the roof top deck even though it was January, and the line at the bar shortened. Steve held back until it died down a bit, talking to Sam Beck, an old college acquaintance, now an insurance agent with Prudential. When the line shortened, he slipped behind a girl with shoulder-length blond hair and a nice figure in a tan dress, slightly shorter than his six-foot three frame.

As she ordered her drink, she turned around and tripped on her toe for a split second, spilling just a bit of her drink on his shirt.

"Oh my God, I'm so sorry," she put her other hand to her mouth.

"No big deal," he smiled. "It's an old shirt. If it cleans up, that's fine. If not, I won't miss it."

She had a smile that would light up any room and sparkling blue eyes he couldn't look away from, almost glittery, with long black lashes and flecks, which were also black but looked like gold to him.

"Well, that's a relief," she smiled back. "I mean, I'm still very sorry, clumsy of me and all." She looked down, "New shoes and they're not quite..."

"Broken in?" he asked, looking directly into those eyes. He was a sucker for eyes. Always had been. These he was getting lost in.

"Yes. I'd say so."

What a smile, combined with those eyes. "I'm Steve, Steve Kaufman," but he didn't hold out his hand, he just kept looking at her.

"Becky Dean," she said, reaching her hand towards him. "When did you graduate?"

Then he took her hand. To hold for a second, not to shake it. "71. You?"

"73. Then for an M.A., also at U of I, in social work."

"Wow, I admire that. I went on for a master's in management at Northwestern. Do you work for an agency or something?"

"Nope. State of Illinois. Department of Human Services."

"I'm a banker at a small bank on the northwest side."

"We'd better move out of the way," she said as she put her hand on his back, and they walked out to the roof top patio railing. They talked the rest of the night until they were almost the last ones there. She had been engaged a few years back, but then her mom became sick, and her dad had already passed, so it was work and then straight home to care for her. Then she was reengaged to the same guy who had since been divorced, but she said he had changed, that he was bitter and frustrated from that marriage and she didn't like what she saw.

He told his story of dating through the years and how it was probably corny, but that he had always looked for a "spark" so to speak. Not a love at first sight scenario, but just that "you'd know." He said it was like that line from the song, something about stars and light, seeing one but not the other. He again thought that was really cliched, but she smiled and nodded.

"The Eagles," she said.

"You got it," he replied. I like this girl, I really do.

She told him how a friend she worked with was Indian and that she was engaged in an arranged marriage and how shocked everyone was. But the girl went on to explain that this was a situation where hopefully through the years they would fall *in* love, instead of marrying when you were supposedly maybe madly in love and then through time fall *out* of love. She said it actually made some sense to her, and then he smiled and nodded, never taking his eyes off her.

She was pretty and obviously intelligent. Her mom passed a few months ago, so she wanted to make up for lost time. The incredible part of all this was that she also lived in Sandburg Village, one building over.

He asked if he could call her and that was it. They were married three months later and although her dad had been Jewish but not her mom, they married in a synagogue. Her brother Eric gave her away and they had their reception at the Hyatt in Rosemont. They found an apartment in Evanston near the CTA Evanston Express and Northwestern commuter line to go downtown.

She had urged him to quit the bank instead of complaining about it all the time and he did, finding a job at Columbia National Bank and Trust on LaSalle Street, one of the largest in the city. He was a junior V.P. so his title went down, but his pay went up, way up. It was now 1981. He was thirty-one, she was twenty-eight, and the future looked bright.

Except they wanted kids. She had made a joke that if they couldn't have kids, she wanted dogs. It became a running joke between them. They tried and tried. Fertility doctors, drugs, nothing worked.

But the doctors, who had probed and prodded and given her every test known to man and woman, noticed something else. And by then it was too late for kids, too late for anything.

A nurse entered the bathroom, nudged him, and helped

him off the floor. She asked if he wanted to stay in the room for the night, against hospital rules, but under the circumstances it would be permitted, as the cancer did its damage in her final hours. He nodded, and she led him to the worn vinyl armchair near the bed, where he closed his eyes and promptly fell asleep.

He was awakened about three a.m. by a different nurse, who gently told him she was gone and asked if he would like to stay in the room a little while longer or even the rest of the night if he wanted. This he did, and then closed his eyes for a deep sleep.

CHAPTER TWO

T he funeral and events surrounding her death were a surreal blur. He went to the funeral home with his parents who had flown in from their home in Ft. Lauderdale and her brother to pick out the casket and make the final arrangements for the chapel for his bride who always said you must have faith even in the darkest hours when all seems hopeless. Why, oh, why are these people, the angelic ones who believe and never seem to do wrong, who never have an unkind word about anyone or anything, taken from us too soon? Is it simply answered by the platitude that his mother used to say so many years ago when her close friend Jeanne Durschlag died, that God takes the angels first?

His parents' rabbi stopped at her brother's house to take down remarks for the funeral, a middle-aged man, heavy set with just a few strands of gray hair peeking through a fedora, a man he thought, who had probably done this so many times it seemed automatic but who had to give each family attention and make it seem special to the bereaved.

He felt himself breathing heavily, the living room hot enough already. He looked at the man with scorn, thinking, "Well guess what, holy man? You've got a hell of a job to do in this case. It isn't every day that my beautiful wife passes away so young and in such profound agony. It's gonna be tough to console everyone, especially me, and you've got a lot of explaining to do on behalf of your Master as well."

He found that despite wanting to take the little notebook Rabbi Tuchman carried to jot down the facts and reminisces about her and either shove it up his ass or down his throat with its deep eastern European accent, his anger temporarily passed as the man spoke in a soft, somber voice that was almost reassuring that everything would ultimately be all right.

He still came to tears when recalling her gentle ways and used an example of how a small mutt had run up to them one time outside their Evanston apartment with a menacing growl, only to start whimpering and rubbing against her leg when she opened her arms and cooed to it like only its mother could do. She had always wanted a dog.

Or the time she thought she lost her keys when they were lodged in her woolen cap that she was wearing, only to become hysterical with that infectious laugh at realizing they were on top of her head.

The rabbi smiled at the stories, jotting away. He asked if the husband wanted to say any words at the funeral, in addition to his own eulogy. Steve shook his head firmly. "I couldn't. To be honest, no one could do her justice with their words."

"Then I'll try Steven. That's all any of us can do."

The condolence calls were made at her brother's house in Lincolnwood, where the cars lined the street and were packed into the double driveway in front of the large, split-level house where Becky Dean had grown up.

Steve's brother had flown in from Vegas, where he had a Cadillac dealership, putting his degree from Rutgers to good use. They hadn't spoken in months. His brother was outgoing and always had a joke. He couldn't deal with that for the last few months, and his brother had finally gotten the message.

Then his old best friend, Jeff Hirsh, came in with his wife.

8

He had been close with Jeff since grade school, and it almost felt at times like they were brothers. But Steve had grown distant from him the last couple of years because he was jealous. Jeff's wife had just had their second child while Becky and Steve had struggled to have any kids and now, she was gone. Steve knew it was wrong, but he still felt that way. They embraced and Jeff suddenly started tearing up, which led Steve to do the same.

Everything seemed surreal, a whirlwind. Marsha and David Kaufman were in from Fort Lauderdale, his mother hugging him for what seemed to be ten minutes and even his father gave him a long embrace, a man not prone to displays of affection.

The guys from work showed up, Al, Stu, and Jack. He talked to them awhile because he was comfortable around them, even though the subject of conversation was obvious. He also wanted to make sure they were at ease because they knew no one there.

Then it happened. Steve had said little to anyone unless approached, sort of wandering through the house, still in a daze, a sort of fog present between him and everyone else. Sometimes voices appeared to be echoes. But this was different. Steve overheard an uncle of Becky's at the dining room table trying to console a young niece of Becky's.

"You must understand that this is His will, that it happened. Some divine reason that we mortals can't understand, even the wisest of sages and prophets."

That did it. Steve could take no more. He glared at the little man in his rumpled suit and outlandishly wide, too short tie, getting directly in his face and restraining himself from grabbing the tie near his throat.

"His will? This is 1981 A.D., not 1981 B.C. What fucking moron would honestly believe that God would take a young, innocent girl for *any* justifiable reason for some master plan?

Maybe some masterbater's plan, if any. If your God is there at all."
He stormed out of the room before a reply or able to observe the
open mouths, gasps, and remarks of those who overheard the
rant and he realized he hadn't scored any points with the Dean
family or anyone else but who really gave a rat's ass?

What did this rumpled suit man know of a couple that had
known each other who were madly in love, two kindred spirits,
soulmates who could answer the other's questions before they
formed them into words, and was now just one, broken spirit
who believed in nothing and again, back from his college days,
questioned everything.

He would go home each night now after a Shiva of three
days and sleep on the couch in the apartment, vowing to never
sleep in their bed again, touching nothing of hers and only
entering the bedroom to get his own clothes and things.

When the days of mourning had passed, and his head
began to clear, he wondered about his life and what was to come.
Would he go back to work? Keep the apartment or move away?
Move far away? Would he ever see certain people again? He
hadn't spoken to his parents since being at the house on the last
night, nor his brother who were both back in Florida and Vegas,
respectively. The phone had rung many times, but he had not
answered it.

There were certain friends and cousins, although very
few, who never showed up at the funeral or paid a condolence
call over the three days. That was easy. Fuck 'em. Other closer
friends and relatives would probably give him some time, then
call to express regrets again and see how he was doing, even
trying to fix him up as time went by. Fuck them too. He was
convinced that to be alone was the best medicine, at least for
now.

It had been almost a week now since the funeral and he
had assiduously avoided contact with every human being that

he possibly could. He needed food, but even wanted to avoid going to the store. This was becoming truly scary. He had never really been alone in his entire life. Growing up in West Ridge, a very nice Chicago neighborhood on the far north side with his parents and brother, then college at Illinois downstate, first in the frat house and then an apartment off campus with roommates. Then with a roommate in the apartment in Sandburg Village not far from downtown Chicago who had just left for L.A. a few months back, and finally with Becky here at the apartment in Evanston.

I can hack it, he thought. After all, he and Becky split the shopping, and he paid the bills. He was a banker, for Christ's sake. Yeah, she kept the house and picked the furniture, but that won't be so hard now. Except her things. God, he couldn't bear to look at her clothes or little knick-knacks or anywhere else her impressions were, from the Nierman print she picked out for the hallway to the hokey needlepoints to her towels or stuffed bears-God, it's too much.

It was the first call he made to his brother-in-law, Eric. "Hey Eric, yeah, I know it's been a while. I'm just trying to process everything and I'm doing a shit job of it. Listen, I want you to come by the place. Bring some help if you want, whenever you want. I want you to take Becky's things. Everything, if you want them or not, just bring them back to the house for now, anyway. Please." There was silence on the phone, then an okay, Eric asking if Sunday morning would work.

"Sure," Steve replied. "Where am I going? Like I said, it's just for now. Yeah, I've thought about it. I have my memories and that's enough. Everything else, lifting a spoon, taking out the trash, just signing the pre-printed thank you cards to come, it's all just painful." Thank goodness, Eric understood.

But fifteen minutes later, his mother called. After admonishing him for not picking up the phone in almost a week, she continued as only Marsha Kaufman, in that slightly high-pitched nasal voice, could. "We've all called you, your father and I, your brother, your friends, your cousins, everyone, and you don't answer. We worry, it's not right, it's not you."

He breathed deeply as his lips quivered. "I just wanted to be alone for a while, that's all. I'm fine, really, I'm telling you. I just hung up with Eric and he's coming to get Becky's things on Sunday." He knew that couldn't be left alone.

"Steven, are you sure about this? You want to block out everything now, I see that, but you can't honey. You're always going to have memories. There's nothing you can do about it."

"Well, right now I want everything out. And Eric is storing most of it in his garage and basement, so if I'm making a hasty decision, it's not like the stuff is gone forever." He knew she always had to be the last one to end a conversation, and he wasn't going to allow it, not this time. "Listen mom, I gotta run to the pharmacy before they close," and he hung up.

He walked down to a bar he knew near the Northwestern campus where he had been some months before with the guys from work. The NCAA tournament was on the tube, but he was half paying attention to it. He had a couple beers and sat staring into space in the crowded, noisy place where he never felt more alone in his entire life. When he returned to the apartment, there was an envelope with his name on it taped to the mailboxes in the front area of the building. When he opened it, he saw a plain note, unsigned, which simply asked him to please answer his phone.

CHAPTER THREE

It was twilight in the alley in the Logan Square neighborhood, with a typical March gray Chicago sky and just a few small patches of snow here and there to remind everyone that winter was still here. Usually, you could hear the sounds of the neighborhood, the televisions and boom boxes flooding the alley with a cacophony from open window cracks and the traffic from the streets at either end where more music would emanate from customized cars with special bass woofers that vibrated or from the rumbling CTA buses. But in winter, there was an eerie silence except for the occasional horn honking or siren.

Hector Astasia stood beneath an alley telephone pole next to a small mound of dirty snow from an old February storm. He was nervously puffing on a cigarette, wearing an old black leather jacket that was too short for even his five-foot frame, and not nearly warm enough to keep out the wind that was starting to blow the loose trash in the alley against the old frame garages. He would periodically shiver and then puff on the cigarette in a sort of awkward set of repetitive motions.

He thought about the past, how at age fifteen he was put on an airplane to be a "mule" or "body packer", stuffing five or ten gram tiny plastic bags down his throat and swallowing them in an airport restroom, being sick on the plane all the way to LA or Chicago where he would wait through customs and then be whisked away to a basement flat, down a strong laxative or ipecac syrup and retrieve the bags for his family, for the precious white.

After about fifteen minutes it was totally dark, and Hector could see the headlights of a car turning down the narrow alley moving slowly. As the car came closer, he recognized the maroon Chevy Monte Carlo belonging to his cousin, Antonio Rendon. The car stopped about ten feet from him, and the headlights were turned off, but the engine was still running. Antonio Rendon slowly emerged from the driver's side while another man quickly came out from the passenger's side, leaning on the door.

Hector was not just shivering from the cold anymore. "Hey, Tonyo, what's up?" he said in a quavering voice, knowing what the men had come for.

Antonio spit on the ground next to him. Not a good sign. He too had on a leather jacket with his hands buried in his pockets as he shifted his weight from side to side. "You know what's up, Hector. The blow never got to Marcus in the burbs. This is times two for you, just like that bullshit last year when you said the law, or the Crescents, were chasing you and you had to ditch it in the trash."

The other man, also with his hands in his pockets, was looking away down the alley, almost seeming to be bored by the conversation.

"No, no, it's not like that," Hector raised his voice, which was now trembling, like the rest of him. "I was supposed to see Marcus at that forest preserve in Niles or wherever the fuck it was, but man, Marcus didn't show; he sent his cousin Edgar instead and I..."

"Oh, so you just GAVE what you had to this guy just like that with no questions asked and figuring it was already paid for, you just walked away. Did you even know him?"

"Yeah, sure, sure. I'd seen him around before, he was…"

"Look," Antonio was now almost yelling, a bad sign. "You fucked up, man. Just admit it. You're family to me and my brothers, but you fucked up. The blow never got to Marcus, and no one knows where it is or who this Edgar is. Bought and paid for! One Kilo. Fifty G. How stupid can you be?!"

Hector said nothing, hanging his head and looking sheepish. Finally, he whispered. "I'm sorry man, I thought he checked out. I've seen him around. I swear on my mother's grave I'll find him and cap him," then thinking that wasn't enough, he added, "And I'll get the white back."

"Hector, Hector," putting his arm on his shoulder and squeezing it affectionately. "You may find him, but how are you going to get anything back? It's probably up seventy Anglos' noses by now. Let's figure this out another way. You meet us tomorrow at Carlos' place. We gotta figure out what to do, comprende?" Antonio's voice was calm now, reassuring.

"Sure, sure Tonyo, what time and I come?" He felt better. The knot in his stomach was easing.

"We'll call you in the morning." Antonio had turned around walking towards the car.

"Gracias!" Hector yelled as he stepped forward, waving his hand.

Antonio nodded to the man by the car, who pulled out a sawed-off shotgun from behind him and leveled a blast into Hector's chest. The blast shattered the silence of the night and propelled Hector against a garage door, where he slumped over. Antonio wheeled around from the driver's side and pulled out a silver-plated pearl handled .45 caliber automatic from his jacket and walked up to the slumping body. Pulling back his head by the hair, he fired two shots into his forehead.

The men walked quickly back to the car, which hurtled

down the alley, tires squealing as they emerged and turned onto the street. The other man was now driving. The car pulled up to a phone booth on Kedzie Avenue, and Antonio got out and placed a phone call.

"Si," answered a voice at the other end.

"It's done," replied Antonio. He hung up and reentered the car, which sped south down the street into the night.

CHAPTER FOUR

Steve went back to work that next week. He was still angry with everyone, especially God, questioning His existence and the world at large, but now it was a cool, just below the surface type of anger of which he was conscious of all the time. He was brought up to believe, then he questioned everything in college, added to by the death of his first true love thirteen years ago, Lily Stibic, who did believe and despite his agnostic leanings, had guided his moral compass for all this time with the idea that he had an inner faith, bolstered by being married to a true believer and absolute optimist. Now all he could say was it didn't do her any good.

Work at the bank was slow. He was a big bank loan officer at a time when the corporate loan rate for his developer borrowers was hovering near eighteen percent. The prime rate had increased six times since the start of 1980, and it was only March of 81'. He was now on the loan committee, but there was not much to discuss when it met on Thursdays.

The first morning, he went through the mail, shuffled through correspondence and made a few calls to existing customers who had called to give their condolences. It was painful. He scribbled some cliches down to say to each of them so he would sound solemn and a bit witty and not have to make up a new conversation each time.

When lunch came around, his office buddies stopped by his desk. They usually ate at the bank's cafeteria unless they were taking out customers or otherwise doing something. Al Burns and Jack (called "Black Jack") Griffin were two other loan officers, Burns being junior and Griffin senior to Steve. Stu Fine, up in the legal department, rounded out the crew.

Burns came up the hard way, dropping out of DePaul after his sophomore year when he began his work career for a telemarketing outfit, a boiler room operation over on west Jackson Boulevard, then starting as a messenger for the bank when he couldn't stand the cold calling anymore, working his way up to loan processor and then loan officer with his bright wit and handsome smile. His customers loved him, as he was incredibly loyal and personable.

Black Jack Griffin was five feet five, had gone to Vandy and was just about to finish his MBA at Northwestern in an after-hours program. Jack was the ultimate WASP banker with dark good looks, blue blazer, and a different regimental stripe tie for every day of the week.

Stu Fine had gone to Indiana, then law school in Champaign. He's tall and wiry like Steve but with red hair, freckles and wire rims. He had come to hate the law department at the bank and its pompous staff; hence, he hung out with the loan officers while itching to get into private practice.

The bank cafeteria food was actually pretty decent for a company cafeteria and, being subsidized, the price was right. Steve piled up his tray, not knowing what lay in store for dinner. They would talk about what guys talk about in their late twenties or early thirties: sports, sex and gripes at work. Everyone tried to avoid the obvious subject with Steve. All of them had been to the funeral and paid their condolences and felt it was best to leave it at that. Before her death, they had also started to talk about various ways of getting high. The conversation ultimately turned to this.

"I heard it was really snowing at Kramer's bachelor party last week," Burns started. "Klein, Wosniak, Bell, the whole Wilmette branch, everybody tooting, doing lines at Kramer's brother's place up in Glencoe."

After the "reallys" and "no shits" replies, Fine chimed in. He had been silent for most of lunch, reflecting his recent moodiness. "That's nothing. You won't believe this." He looks around and then leans in. The others join. "Friday, I'm wrapping up some research on this claim we got in. We're gonna give it to outside counsel, and I wanted to run something by Cremmons. So, I go down to his office. I wasn't even sure he'd be in; it was almost six. His door was slightly open, and I peered in. There he is, leaning over his desk and on the glass top he's snorting powder, a thin trail at least six inches long. The Associate General Counsel for the whole goddamned bank! I freaked out and ran." More "reallys" and "no shits."

"Where is everyone getting this stuff from?" asks Griffin. I know it's all over the west coast, but it's supposed to be so expensive and with inflation and everything..."

Burns, who started the whole conversation, cuts him off and changes the subject, squirming to mention a hot investment tip he heard about, but Steve is intrigued about the previous conversation and brings it back. "Aren't like the street gangs dealing it and spreading it around, like always? I mean, gangs have been dealing drugs for years, since the Mob had this hands-off policy about them."

"Yes, but Steve, drug dealing on this scale is a big, expensive business. International cartel business through Columbia, Peru, and Mexico as the entry points. The gangs aren't big enough or rich enough to handle that type of operation, especially in poor neighborhoods where they came from," said Stu, with his attorney's aura of authority. "They simply can't afford the blow."

They all realized it was getting late as Jack looked at his watch and they all scurried to the elevator to get back upstairs. Steve knocked off early, begging off going to a sports bar with Al, who had a miserable marriage and didn't want to go home.

Steve was in the elevator thinking about how she always had dinner ready when he came home, even if she had worked late at Lyttons in Old Orchard on weekends and the traffic was a mess to Evanston. Now he would try cooking for himself, at least for tonight. Hell, it looked easy.

He found a box of pasta and put it in a pot of water on a high flame, fumbling through the cabinets for some meat sauce to add. Meanwhile, he snapped on the TV to catch a Trapper John, MD. episode which he got lost in. After entering the kitchen to find the pasta boiling over and broken into tiny pieces from being overcooked, he swore in disgust and headed out the door down a couple of blocks to grab a pizza at a corner restaurant.

CHAPTER FIVE

Manuel Cruz realized he was late after he left the car with the valet in front of the condo hi-rise on Lake Shore Drive. The doorman recognized him and gave him a nod as he rushed to catch an elevator about to close to the twenty-second floor. The apartment door was open, and he let himself in. The two other men were already seated in the living room, hunched over a glass table facing each other, pouring through figures in a large ledger book. Carlos Rendon yelled to him, although they were just a few feet away. "Manny, you're late. Traffic or a woman, eh?"

"Si Carlos, a woman. A big fat mamaceta with no teeth. She says she knows you." Smirks from Carlos and the other man.

"Sit cuz," Carlos replied, "and we'll go over the good and bad news together." Carlos was a large man with a broad, dark face and a wide space between his front teeth, his hair pulled back in a ponytail, which he only tied at home or amongst friends.

His brother Antonio was the other man. Slight and good looking, he could pass for White and was dressed impeccably in a dark silk suit with a tie and matching kerchief.

Manuel was their first cousin and, as much as he loved his cousins, he was nervous around them. They had always been good to him and he to them, helping to handle the day-to-day affairs of one of the largest cocaine distribution operations in Chicago.

As Manuel settled into a Barcelona chair set on a white fur rug between the brothers, Carlos sighed and continued. "Compadres, we are in good shape in the Loop and north side and in the western suburbs, all the way out to Aurora. Our friends out on Roosevelt Road have been moving fifty kilos every two weeks. The basement of the church is perfect; shit, we could set up another lab there if things keep up like this. But we have a weak link, and we all know what it is, si?" He paused for a few seconds. The others knew what it was, but out of respect, they would let him continue.

"The northern burbs are a disaster. The narcs have joined with the local law from Evanston, Skokie, Wilmette, all the way up to Lake County and they are breathing down our necks. This new FBI honcho, Webster, means business. Surveillance, informers, and arrests can't be far off if we're not careful. Hector Astasia thought he could be a runner *and* handle operations after deliveries, and he couldn't do either. Then he starts skimming and finally steals shipments. We still got our people in place up there, but we gotta have someone take charge, someone we trust. Manny, I think, amigo, it's gotta be you until we can bring someone up."

There is silence for a minute. Manual had known this was coming and was not thrilled with the idea of finding a new place to live in the suburbs where he would have to relocate to keep a constant watch on matters. He was a city boy, first in Matamoros and now here in Chicago in Little Village. But he knew he couldn't refuse. "Okay Carlos. I'll start hanging out up there and look for a casa."

Carlos looked at him with those dark eyes that seemed to go right through you. "I know this is hard to do. Your family is in the city, I know. But Manny, the Anglos in the northern burbs are our second biggest customers after Aurora. We're a poco piss ant operation if we lose this."

"We still need a runner or two up there with Hector gone," added Antonio.

"We'll let Manny get set up there and see what he thinks. Hopefully, he finds someone in the family or someone up there he can trust, who lives there. But we gotta move fast," Carlos replied, stabbing his finger on the ledger book. "We're losing thousands and thousands a week up there now, more every day with the white reaching two g's an ounce. Everyone's paying $100 a gram and it's like this inflation shit, my friends, it's only going higher."

"Okay, let me settle in and we'll start the mule train running again," answered Manny. "Where's Angie?"

"You and my sister," Carlos smiled broadly. "You still got the hots for her after all these years. She's in the laundry room. Came over to help me with it."

"No," Manuel replied, trying to show little emotion, and refusing to be teased. "My mother just wanted to know if she was coming to Anita's communion next Sunday."

"She should be back in a few, then you can ask her yourself." Carlos was trying to goad him. He knew Manuel was shy and uncomfortable around her, that he had always had a crush on her since they were kids, but she had publicly proclaimed she would only marry someone very, very special and, after all, they were cousins.

"No, it's okay, she'll call her." He then spied a set of car keys on a glass sculptured table next to the chairs. "Those look like Hector's Trans Am keys."

"You got it baby," said Carlos. "You want the wheels? If not, one of the family will take it."

"Na, it's too out there for me. Everyone knows who you are

in that thing."

"And knows you're coming," added Antonio.

They all laughed, but it was a nervous, almost forced laugh. They knew Hector's fate. Yes, he was family. But he was stupid and, worse, greedy. Hiding the blow for a while now and not covering his moves very well. That's what got him iced. But in this business, it's hard not to get greedy. "I like my 300 Benz. It ain't so new, but it gets me around. And the compartments I have in it are tough to find if I'm carrying product."

"Si Manny. We all know about your movable rocker panels," Carlos smiled. More laughter, more genuine this time.

The meeting broke up and Manuel heaved a sigh of relief in the elevator, looking at his thin, tired face in a mirror panel which belied the fact that he was only thirty-five years old. All this business was aging him quickly. He thought it was going to be a long year, and it was only March as the parking garage valet went to retrieve his car and he gazed at the cold, dark sky out over Lake Michigan.

CHAPTER SIX

Steve's mother, Marsha, has two sisters. One is Shirl, a widow who lives in a condo in Highland Park. The other is Edith, married to Bernie, who lives in a home in Morton Grove. Steve saw them at the funeral. Before that he hadn't seen them in months, but now his mother was urging him to see more of them since she lives in Florida and firmly believes he has to maintain a connection with family during this time when everyone is worried about him. She believes they could almost be surrogate parents to her troubled son, especially since they had no children.

So, unbeknownst to Steve, his mother had called Edith and asked if she could have him over for that Friday at the end of his second week back at work. Edith had called him that Sunday before, caught him off guard, and he obliged.

Now he dreaded this. He was tired after taking the train home from the office and walking home from the Main Street station. He hadn't been sleeping well and had a headache which centered over one eye. After downing three aspirin and lying down for a minute, he got up and changed, trying to remember where he put his car keys. When he found them, he had to laugh and almost sob at the same time when he thought of the number of times Becky had scolded him for not remembering where he put things while she did the same thing more often than he did.

The 79' Cutlass needed a wash from winter's grime and road salt on the streets. As he started the car, he thought about subleasing the apartment until May when the lease was up and moving near north in the city, just to get rid of all the memories that uncontrollably enter his mind, whether waking or sleeping. The song on the radio "In the City," by the Eagles, only bolstered his sentiments.

The house in Morton Grove seemed timeless, outside and inside. His aunt Edith hugged him hard as he entered. She was small and gray but still had her sparkling blue eyes behind her half glasses, not unlike his wife. Steve remembered when they were once very close, closer than he had ever been to his uncle. She just seemed easier to talk to about school, work, girls, marriage, just about anything except sports and politics. That was primarily left to Bernie, who had an opinion about everything, which is why Steve limited their discussions to small talk. Tonight, he hopefully thought, would be no exception, and that was just fine.

"Where's Uncle Bernie"?

"He's in the den watching the news."

"Stevie, sit, sit," his uncle motioned him to the couch. "Edith, are we ready to eat?"

This was good. He had to spend limited time with him alone.

"In a few minutes Bernie, the brisket's almost done."

"So how have you been?" he asked, pushing his reading glasses up on his balding forehead. "The bank treating you okay?"

"Yeah, I guess. I'm just getting back into things, but there's not much business loan activity. It's kind of dried up."

"Well, sure it has. Inflation at eighteen percent, people

upset over gas prices. Carter can't get our people out of Iran. Who wants to invest in anything these days?"

Steve smiled. Same old Bernie. Knows it all, sure of everything. It's black or white. The man enlisted in the Marines at seventeen, lied about his age. His family thought he was crazy, a young Jewish kid going off to war and with the Marines, of all things. But he wanted to see more than the west side of Chicago. So, he was at Guadalcanal and Okinawa. Still had that barrel chest with the mounds of hair and the stocky but sturdy frame of a man twenty years younger. Steve spotted two books on a table next to Bernie's lounge chair, "The Devil's Alternative" and "Jailbird". "You reading those?" he pointed.

"Na, they're your aunt's. From her book club. I did read a Vonnegut book once. Bet you can't guess which one college man."

Steve pondered the question for a second. "Slaughterhouse Five," he proudly answered. "Because it had World War Two in it."

"You got it," laughed his uncle. "Though the rest of it was crap." He got up slowly from his chair, firmly placing his big hands on the arms to boost himself up. Although his aunt hadn't called that it was ready, he looked straight ahead, "let's eat."

Dinner was more small talk. John Wayne Gacy's trial and conviction, the primary election coming up for States' Attorney with Richie Daley, and the NCAA basketball tournament. Gas was going over a dollar thirty a gallon. But Edith Morris wanted to bring the conversation back to personal matters, like a bee circling a flower until it finally lands.

"Steven, you've got to start living again. I know, we all know you've been in a daze and God knows, who could blame you, but it's time to come out. You haven't called anyone or returned calls. Everyone's concerned about you."

"Aunt Edith, please. I didn't come over here for this. All I want is just some peace and quiet and a good meal."

"Stevie," his uncle countered, "I want to hear it from you, not family or friends. How do YOU feel? Are you depressed, lonely, what? Talk to us."

"No, if you want to know the truth, I'm simply bitter. Yeah, that will sum it up in a nutshell. I'm bitter. Why Becky and why not me or you? Can you tell me that? Cause no one else can. Not your psychologists or rabbis or Dear Abbeys. No one."

"Stevie, if I knew why you or why this one or that one, hell, I'd be famous, on TV. No one knows why. You're smart enough to know that." He crossed his arms, serious now for the first time, satisfied with what he had said.

With teeth clenched, Steven replies, "Well I want answers, damnit. I deserve answers."

"Look, no one deserves anything," Bernie almost yells. "We talked about this when we were sitting Shiva. Nobody knows why and if they did..."

"The point is you're asking for something no one knows but, in the meantime, you still have to move on," Edith calmly says as she puts her hand on his wrist.

"I'm well aware of that. It'll take some more time, but we'll see. How's Aunt Shirl?" he asked, changing the subject.

"Oh, the same. She asked about you the other day." It worked. The rest of the night was spent on small talk again. He left just before the ten o'clock news.

The rest of the weekend was quiet. Saturday night he went out with a second cousin, Roger, who lived in Evanston and was a grad student at Northwestern. They went to the Evanston theater to see The Electric Horseman for a dollar fifty, then to an all-night diner. He still slept on the couch but needed to change the sheets in the worst way. He had gotten into the habit of opening the mail every few days instead of every day as Becky would have done, just as he would walk around the apartment with his shoes on, something she never would have allowed. In some sort of perverse way, he thought these were small rebellions against her death, that he'd show her that he would do what he wanted, that no one could interfere, that if she was still here, he wouldn't do these things, but the fact was she wasn't, so there. Fuck it.

Going through the stack of mail Sunday morning after tossing out all the ads and putting the bills aside, he opened a long, handwritten letter from his brother-in-law Eric, begging him to keep in contact with him and that possibly by doing so a sort of dual healing could be achieved. He started to crumple up the letter to toss it away, but stopped at the last minute and stuck it in a kitchen drawer on top of the rubber bands and appliance warranties.

He was never a person to feel sorry for himself for long, remembering an incident long ago in little league when his team lost the championship and a friend on the team, Larry Arbeiter, was sullen about the loss for weeks. He yelled at him, saying they deserved to lose. They played like shit and to just move on. Just like Edith said Friday night, except more tactfully. Granted, this loss was far greater, but he was out of tears, emotionally wrung out, and ready for whatever was next.

That night, he decided to sleep in the bedroom for the first time. He changed the sheets, plopped into bed in his underwear and figured I'm tired, so be it. My back deserves a rest from that damn sofa.

CHAPTER SEVEN

Manuel Cruz was becoming increasingly impatient, pacing in his apartment in Little Village while he waited for his younger brother Jesus. He was never on time and was probably holed up at the Cinestage or some other adult theater where he spent most of his free time when not serving as a runner for the ring. Little shit, Manuel thought. I raised him with no father around and gave him a job and helped him get on his feet after he does time, and he spits on me.

He waited another ten minutes then bounded down the front stairs and sped off with the real estate section of the Tribune to look for some new digs on the far north side or in the north burbs where Carlos wanted him to set up shop and run things for the north. He had a street map with him as well, since he wasn't at all familiar with the area anywhere north of Lawrence Avenue in the city.

Manuel had been the head of his family, taking care of his brother and two younger sisters and their mother for as long as he could remember. It hadn't been easy coming up from Matamoros with a father who left them when he was seven, dropping out of school, doing menial odd jobs until his cousin Carlos was up in the states, hiring him to bring drugs into El Paso from across the border by car. He was well aware that laws were being broken, but the family had to eat and his mother didn't make nearly enough to feed and clothe them all as a maid in a fleabag motel.

Now he was making what could be considered a fortune, even if he had landed in jail for a stretch of months on and off for possession. Still, someday he dreamed of getting out, of owning a small business like a restaurant or video store and settling down to marriage and a family. He reasoned this life now could not go on forever, either the police or the other gangs who Carlos had an uneasy truce with would close in. Then he would end up either busted or even dead. So why not now? The question was not an easy one to answer, if there even was an answer.

He worked his way driving north and then west into the eastern part of Skokie near the sanitary district plant off McCormick Boulevard, where there were neat little houses when he spotted an address for an open house from the Tribune. It was a small, well-maintained brick ranch.

The real estate lady who greeted him at the door was obviously reluctant to give him the grand tour, even though he was neatly dressed in a tapered leather jacket, silk sport shirt and slacks with Gucci loafers. Wrong race. Wrong place. But she bit her lip and showed him the three bedrooms and bath and a half with a rather large unfinished basement where he saw no water marks. He liked it. There was no furniture; the couple who owned it had been transferred out of state and had a hard time selling with interest rates so high and inflation out of control. The price had been lowered three times to eighty thousand.

"Would you like to leave your name in our register book?" she asked, believing, or hoping, he was just passing through.

"I like it and I think I'll take it," he seriously replied, looking towards a small park across the street.

"Well, there is the mortgage qualification and the contract which has to be drawn up for..."

"A mortgage won't be necessary. As for the contract, you

draw it up and call me to come out and sign it," he said, handing her a business card which simply had his name and phone number. Her mouth was agape.

"Well Mr. Cruz," she stuttered as she looked at the card, not believing what was happening. "It is customary to leave an earnest money deposit, to show good faith, so to speak."

"Fine, how much?"

"Well, ultimately ten percent total is customary but if it will be a cash closing with no mortgage, five percent is fine until the house is inspected and if it passes inspection, then it would …"

"Five percent, four thousand. Right?"

She is about to pinch herself, figuring she will then wake up, but replies, "Yes, if you want me to write up a judgment note for that amount or if you have a personal check, I can…"

"No, here, I'll give it to you right now," as he reaches into a stuffed alligator wallet and counts out twenty-one-hundred-dollar bills and goes into his pocket for another twenty, hundred dollar bills. There is a visible shake in her hands as she takes the bills and walks over to a card table set up in the living room and writes out a receipt for him, a slight smile across his lips as he watches. After handing him the receipt she explains that the form contracts were back at her office but that she would make one out later that day and call him to come back and review it with her and sign it to present to the sellers unless he wanted his lawyer to look at it to which he shook his head.

"We didn't discuss a closing date and possession," as she looks at him seriously.

"As soon as possible," he replies, again looking at the park across the street. She still seemed in a state of shock as they shook hands and said goodbye.

After he left, he realized he still had to see the Delgados to let them know the latest, that he was going to run things in the north burbs from now on as Hector's replacement. But they already knew that, and they could wait a bit as he walked across the street over by the park, although he didn't want to stay too long. A Latino in this neighborhood, by a park where there were a few kids playing even on a cold March day, that couldn't be good. But as he watched them running around laughing in the crisp March air with a few patches of snow on the brown grass, he thought this was what he truly wanted.

CHAPTER EIGHT

At work on Monday, Steve, Al, Jack, and Stu decided to dine out for burgers at the R Double R about a block away. This was a below street level restaurant which had its famous country western motif with wooden tables that had names and initials carved in them over every square inch of space and a jukebox P.A. system that droned country songs on end, every one of which involved either a girl, a truck, beer or whiskey and Jesus in some combination.

Steve and Stu had the 'Annie Oakley', Al and Jack the 'Cisco', but all the orders looked and kind of tasted the same. While waiting, they again started to discuss who was using. By now, everyone, even straight arrow Jack, had tried it, everyone except for Steve.

"Come on," Al goaded him, "you gotta try it just once. You can't really get hooked on it and heaven knows you could sure use the high."

"Yeah, but hell, I drink. That makes me feel good, gives me a buzz, and elevates my mood, same as this stuff I bet."

"It's nothing like that," said Stu, always sounding imperious. "From just a milligram or two of the really pure stuff, your mood is elevated like with alcohol, but then you have this rush of excitement and feelings of great physical and mental power, as if you can do anything."

"And say you're tired from work or whatever, your fatigue will disappear," added Al, "like that," as he snaps his fingers.

"Where have I been that you guys know all this shit and I don't?"

"Well, you've kind of been out of the loop for a bit, my friend," says Al as he puts his arm around him.

"I have to admit it's all true," says Jack, shaking his head. "I tried it at my cousin's wedding last weekend. We were in a suite at the hotel getting dressed just before the ceremony. All the groomsmen. Six of us fumbling around while my cousin's hogging the bathroom. After about fifteen minutes, we're pounding on the door for him to come out, but he's oblivious to it all. Truth was, he was having the shits, nervous as hell. So, his younger brother pulls out this silver case saying he didn't know about everybody else, but he needed a snort, a toot. He walks over to a table and spills some powder on the glass, spreading it in lines with his fingers and straightening it with the edge of a card in the room which explained how to use the TV. Then he rolls a cigarette paper very carefully into a small tube and snorts one of the lines right up. Before long, everyone joined in and in minutes, we're all in this state of, oh, I don't know, call it bliss. Happy, but like Stu said, you feel you can do anything. The groom ultimately comes out of the bathroom and his brother makes up another line and believe me, that's the only way he got through his own wedding. Never would have made it otherwise."

Just then, one of the chefs blurts out into a microphone over the P.A., "Number one forty-one. Cisco burger."

"That's me," answers Jack, and bolts up to the counter.

"Shit, if a tight ass squid like Jack has tried it, then everyone must know about this," says Steve.

"Well, at this point just about everyone I know *is* an

occasional user," answers Al. "At parties or any type of gathering, it always comes out. Someone always has some."

Knowing Al is a huge sports fan, Steve prods him further. "You mean to tell me that if you're with some guys and you're say watching the NCAA tournament, that this stuff is taking the place of your beer and chips and even the rush you get just from the games?"

"Well yeah," he laughs. "We might start out with beer and such, but then if someone has some coke, we'll go right to that, but it isn't wise to mix the two."

"Then how can you even enjoy the game, follow your Badgers to see if they're winning or losing?" Steve asks. He didn't want to seem prudish, but as a formerly avid sports fan himself until recently, this really bugged him.

Al giggled a bit. "When you start to get high on coke, you really don't care who's winning or losing."

Stu laughed as well. "Yes, and you should see the TV screen on the stuff. It looks like it's moving in and out and the picture is distracted and fragmented but kind of in 3 D or something."

"Yeah, I've noticed that too," replied Al, clearly excited by the shared experience.

They talked about it all through lunch, with the jukebox blaring through the P.A. system, interrupted when an order was ready, wailing songs like "Time after Time" and "Dropkick Me Jesus" (through the Goal Posts of Life). Steve finally agreed to try some that Friday night at a little get together at Stu's place north on State Parkway. They would all be there except for Jack, who had a pre-season meeting for his lacrosse club.

Friday after work, they hailed a cab after having a few drinks and burgers at the Cohasset Punch Bar and Grill on Madison Street near the bank. Rush hour was still not over, and the cab crawled up towards State Parkway to Stu's apartment.

Steve was both mildly excited and apprehensive as to how he would react to what he was about to do.

After everybody settled in and got comfortable on either Stu's couches or the thick rug leaning against the couches, he emerged from his bedroom with a sealed plastic bag which had maybe three or so grams of the white powder. He took great pains to explain to everyone how this was a freebee but that he had paid the going rate of a hundred dollars a gram and if they wanted any more, they would have to pay at least what he had paid. He poured several lines on the glass coffee table in front of one of the couches, each being about a milligram or so, and provided everyone with thin cigarette folding papers. He went first and sniffed one of the lines all at once, holding his other nostril shut. Al followed suit, as did Steve, who only managed to sniff about half of his line when he couldn't breathe any more.

Stu turned on his stereo, which began blaring a cassette of Jimi Hendrix, *Purple Haze*, the haze being the appropriate word. Steve leaned his head back on the couch and after about ten minutes, Al and Stu were describing how they felt, but Steve had experienced no reaction yet except for a little lightheadedness. He was still holding on to the paper tube and reached over to finish his line on the table. As soon as he finished in less than a few minutes, the effects started.

"Hey, I'm finally starting to feel something."

"What's it like?" asked Stu.

"I feel giddy, like just happy, and every muscle in my body wants to move."

"Yeah, anything else?" Al asked?

"It's weird. I remember things from my childhood vividly. A lineball game at the grammar school playground. I can picture every kid, what position he was at, and even what he was wearing!"

"I told you," Al said, "they don't call it a mind-expanding drug for nothing."

"I can feel my heart pounding in my chest and it's beating pretty fast."

"That's very common," said Stu in a matter-of-fact manner.

"It's part of the rush of physical power," added Al, as he reached for and crushed an empty beer can to prove his point.

Colors were vivid to Steve, accompanied by bursts of energy where he felt he needed to go outside the apartment and run up and down the hallway. He had barely touched his burger at dinner and only had about half a beer in the apartment, but he wasn't hungry at all. He guessed that was part of the reaction.

He rationalized that he needed to feel good, feel high: he was entitled to this after what he had been through. And it seemed to work for a short while until he went back in and dozed off, even with the stereo blasting. Because despite everything, he craved sleep most of all, not having slept well since she had gone to the hospital for the last time.

Stu's loud door buzzer rudely woke him up as it did to Al, who was also out while Stu was attempting to clean up the apartment. It was Karen, Al's younger sister, who had agreed to pick up Al and Steve at midnight from a party she was at and drop them off at home, knowing the condition they might be in. She had to owe Al a huge favor to do this, which he would not reveal. They gathered their coats, thanked Stu and dragged themselves to the elevator, looking like they slept in their suits from work, which they had actually done.

Karen greeted them warmly in the lobby, but knew better to ask what they were up to. Al had to direct her to Steve's Evanston apartment because he started to fall asleep again. Still, he could feel every bump in the road, every sound the car would make from the mild squeal of the brakes to the misfire of the engine in the old Dodge as it accelerated onto Lake Shore Drive.

"Well Steve, you gonna do it again?" were Al's parting remarks as he let him out in front of his building after nudging him awake.

"I think I would have enjoyed it better if I hadn't been so tired," he yawned, "but yeah, I think so. It was worth it to feel that good."

He shuffled to his apartment door and fumbled for his keys. He took off his suit and put it on the bed, brushed his teeth and washed his face after checking the answering machine for calls. He grabbed a pillow and blanket from the bedroom and plopped down on the living room couch to watch some TV. Within minutes he was asleep, dreaming about the funeral at the cemetery where he looked towards the sky and saw a kaleidoscope of colors, all very vivid and discernable.

He woke up sweating profusely and checked the time, 2:06. He had been asleep for not even an hour and felt wide awake, like he wanted to do something, anything. He got dressed and decided to take a walk around the block. Before he did, he opened the bedroom window widely as he felt like he was suffocating as he breathed in and out.

The March air outside was crisp and cold, which felt good on his face, but at the same time the darkness seemed to be closing in on him. He thought how he hated winters as the darkness comes early and he felt being crushed, and how it brings death.

Back in the apartment after about twenty minutes, he was calmer but still had feelings of claustrophobia. He went back to the couch, but his thoughts seemed to be racing and finally, when he could stand no more, he fumbled through the bathroom medicine cabinet and found one of her many pain pills which he downed with some water cupped in his hand as he would not touch her cup on the sink and didn't know where his was.

He finally nodded off for a few minutes, thinking about how low he had sunk since the evening started and what she would have said, sure that he actually heard her voice. He felt tears coming, how depressed he was with no one to complain about it to, then pondering that this must be the flipside of the white powder, the dark side they don't tell you about.

He awoke again at 4:30 in another sweat, after a nightmare about being chased by giant bugs whose eyes were on long stalks. His heart was pounding rapidly, and his breathing was rapid and shallow. It must have been thirty degrees outside, but the apartment seemed like a sauna. He threw open the rest of the windows and crawled into a fetal position in the corner of the bedroom with a pillow he cradled as he thought of a main street in a small town somewhere downstate where he was walking alone on a sidewalk at sunset with a cool summer breeze against his face.

CHAPTER NINE

Steve started to see people again, slowly and almost methodically, as he still had his list of who came to the funeral and made a condolence call, who called and who didn't. He started another list, prioritizing those who had called him at the house after a week or so either offering continued condolences, seeing if he needed anything and offering to get together soon. Those people were put on his A list, others who called or paid a condolence call were on the B list.

Anyone else could pound salt, even people who were on vacation or had something else going on. Unless they suddenly called, he would never reach out to them again. I'm bitter, he reasoned, and I have a right to be. So, he started making plans for weekends and even during the week on Thursday evenings, as work was usually slow on Fridays. Except this coming Friday when he would be going to a club after dinner with the gang from work.

He also had to hold open Tuesday, March 18th as his uncle Bernie had asked him to come by the house to watch the primary election on TV, especially the heated battle between Rich Daley and Ed Burke for Cook County State's Attorney. His uncle shared a passion with Steve for local politics, although he was not looking forward to a night of opinionated observations.

Although he had made some plans and now felt it would

do him some good, he was really looking forward to this Friday night more than anything. Stu had been given the name of a club on Rush Street from his buddies at Cardiff & Norcross, who, in addition to deviant sexual encounters, were also now into drugs, particularly cocaine, sometimes engaging in both simultaneously. Stu had said the club did not even have a name on the outside, just an address, and that sometimes other things flowed freely. It sounded dangerous and mysterious to a novice like Steve, but if the others would be there, he wanted to go along.

Becky's cousin Riva had called him during the week to see if he wanted to join her and a friend (he smelled a possible fix up) on Friday to see B.B. King at the Blues Max, a club in the Hyatt near O'Hare airport. She knew he liked the blues, and this was a chance to see the best. But he begged off as the Friday night excursion to the club was no doubt where he would rather be. He thought of the blues and jazz and the many hours he spent at home or in the car, especially with his closest friend from grammar school through college, Jeff Hirsh, listening to jazz and then the blues, going to venues with sometimes only a handful of people. They were good times, but he's moved way, way on, set to go on new adventures.

Friday night couldn't come soon enough. They talked about it every day, at lunch and a couple of times when they went out after work to eat something and watch the NCAA tournament games at a bar on Division Street. At long last Friday arrived and after work they decided to grab some steaks at a downtown restaurant, the Berghoff, courtesy of Al, who had just received a small inheritance from an aunt who died in Kenosha. After that, they hailed a cab and the driver grumbled when Stu mentioned the Rush Street destination as it was apparently too crowded for him although he'd easily be able to pick up fares there, especially on a Friday night.

Even though it was a cold March night, it seemed half the

city was out and walking or driving down Rush Street. Stu had not said much about the club except that it had a small band, you needed an invite to get in, and there was no name on the door. It turned out the two-story structure was wedged in between two other clubs, Billy's and the Backroom, both of which had flashing neon signs blaring at the street.

They climbed the steps, letting Stu lead the way, surrounded by freshly painted wrought iron fencing to a black door with an eyehole. Stu knocked and a large Black man with a shaved head and tinted glasses opened the door and folded his arms across his chest barring the way, waiting for an explanation.

"Arnie sent us," Stu said nervously.

"Sheeit," he replied. "Arnie must have sent ten people here tonight. Come on in, you four ain't gonna make no difference."

He pointed down a dark hallway which led to an area with a coatroom and a thin man standing with slick black hair and a moustache, dressed in an irradiant double-breasted suit. He led them to a small black padded booth, and they scooted in.

"There's a two-drink minimum," he said in a Hispanic accent. "Enjoy."

There was a small bar in the corner and about twenty tables arranged in a semicircle toward a small stage.

Seated at the tables were either mostly male business types, or Latinos, both men and women. Stu thought he recognized several politicians and a judge. Dimmed ceiling lighting except for klieg lights pointing toward the stage made up the total illumination.

A cocktail waitress appeared, a pretty, young, dark-haired girl with a bit too much eye make-up at the corners that made her look like an evil queen in an Italian dubbed Hercules movie.

"What you havin boys?" she cooed in a low voice.

Everyone ordered hard drinks. They had their fill of beers with dinner earlier. Steve immediately noticed a table near the front where three Latino males sat with one ravenous, long-haired woman with her ankles crossed in a dark suede skirt with a slit up the side. Her skin was dark, and her long, sculpted nails nervously stirred a swizzle stick in an almost empty glass. One man was rather large, dressed entirely in black with a wide face, gap-toothed grin and his hair pulled back into a pony tail, the second seemed taller and thinner and was impeccably dressed in a three-piece suit while the third was lighter skinned with handsome features and deep set but sad eyes pulled down at the corners and a razor thin moustache. From their gestures and conversations, although Steve could not hear it, it seemed the large man in black was the authority figure. He could have stared all night at the girl, but given her company, that was definitely not wise.

His concentration was broken by the waitress returning with their drinks, followed by an emcee on stage who appeared to look like a young Caesar Romero in a white linen suit with an ascot around his neck.

"Ladies and gentlemen, senoritas, senoras, and seniors. Club Maravel is proud to present the Latin jazz sounds of Ruben Torres!" he announced with a swoop and flourish of his arm as the stage curtains parted.

"So now we at least know where we're at," Al said, smiling to the group. The six-piece band was very loud in the small club, although the Latin jazz beat quickly took over as the audience started tapping and swaying with the rhythm. A second round of drinks came, and the band finished their first set. Everyone at the table was thinking the same thing. This was a neat place, but so far just another club. The anticipation had been far greater than the event. They made small talk about who some of the patrons were and possibly who owned the club. Was it some cartel? The Outfit? Did politicians have a hand in it?

The band returned for a second set and the songs were slower now, ballad types. A large black woman accompanied them on several songs, and as she crooned a song that had strong hints of the blues, Steve laughed to himself that he had the chance to hear the blues tonight after all.

The group had ordered another round beyond the minimum at the start of the second set; it would have seemed uncool to sit for another hour or so without drinking and they were almost scared not to. Besides, the few meager pretzels and chips that the waitress had brought, which seemed like three hours ago, only added to their thirst which was, of course, the intent. One by one, they got up to relieve themselves, Steve being the last. Al joked that Steve had an iron bladder and there were the usual comments about never owning liquor but merely renting it.

With the very limited lighting, Steve fumbled and felt his way to the men's room, which was just behind the coat check area where they came in. He was lightheaded but not drunk, although when he touched things like the door handle it felt unreal, as if he had to do it again to make sure it had just happened.

While standing at the urinal, the man with the sad eyes who was at the table with the girl walked in and stood next to him at the only other stall.

"Nice place, huh?" he said to Steve.

"Yeah," he sighed. "We're having an okay time, but we thought there'd be a bit more action going on," then thinking he couldn't believe he just said this to a total stranger. It had to be the liquor talking.

"Oh, what were you expecting?" the man coolly replied.

"Well, you know, something more than booze and the

show."

"What like women, perhaps or..."

"No, no, nothing like that. Something to make you feel good." Shit, what was he doing? But he started this conversation and might as well see it through, although if this guy was a cop or something, he'd be in deep shit.

"Oh," the man laughed as if he understood. "Well, that doesn't normally happen just by walking in here, unless something is, how would you say it, prearranged?"

"Yeah, well, the guys I'm with didn't prearrange anything except to get us in here."

"Well, kid, you certainly know how to speak your mind. The name's Manuel, but everyone calls me Manny. I'd normally offer you my hand, but under the circumstances...." They both laughed.

"My name's Steve and I hear ya."

As they moved to the sinks, Manuel pulled something out of his pocket. It appeared to be a small silver vial, no bigger than a thimble, with a cap on it. "Here, so the evening's not a total waste, take a whiff of this," as he unscrewed the top.

Steve closed one nostril and inhaled deeply. "Thanks."

"Just don't mention it to your friends or anyone else. Call it a gift."

Steve smiled and nodded, right before his head felt like it was going to explode. As he looked into the bathroom mirror, it seemed there were incredible colorful shapes all around his head which was grotesquely distorted. None of his features were distinct. He couldn't tell where his eyes ended, and his forehead began. "Wow," was all he could muster while Manuel chuckled. Steve leaned hard against the vanity, then shook his head vigorously and leaned back against the far wall. He felt almost normal again.

"Good stuff, eh? You better stay here a few minutes before going back in. I like you, kid, something about you." He kept smiling all the while. Then he pulled out a business card out of his suit pocket. It simply had his name and number on it and Steve looked at it and shoved it in his pants pocket.

"Thanks," Steve said.

"You ever need more stuff or just want to talk, let me know. Don't worry, I'm not queer or nothin. I got a brother about your age."

"Okay, thanks Manny. I may just do that." He was surprised he remembered his name, given his present condition.

"You have a ride out of here, kid?" he then asked.

"Yeah, my friends out there, or I can still take the commuter train up to Evanston." He scolded himself for telling him where he lived, but then thought that something seemed trustworthy about him, something reassuring. "You live around here?" he then asked, again not believing he was saying the words coming out of his mouth as his brain still seemed to be floating around the room.

"Not too far, down near Little Village, but I'm buying a place in the burbs."

Another man came into the washroom, an older man who Stu pointed out earlier as a judge or prosecutor. This broke up the conversation. "Well, take care, and remember what I said," Manuel turned and said, pushing on the door leading out.

"Yeah, I will. Thanks."

As he made his way back to the table, the band had stopped playing and people were starting to leave. The group was back to discussing the NCAA tournament, a conversation which started in the restaurant.

"You fall in or something?" Al asked.

"No. but I think I'm sick from mixing beer with these mixed drinks, even if they did seem watered down."

"Well let's get going," said Stu. "This was a fucking waste. You guys gonna catch a cab or what?"

"I got my car at a lot on Wells Street, so we just have to get to there," Al replied.

"You cheap asshole," Stu grinned. "Perish the thought you park closer to work for an extra buck or two."

"It's not that. This place is a self-park, and the closer lots have those car jockeys who I don't want scraping my car."

"Dickhead, it's a six-year-old Ford," Cracked Stu.

"Oh, piss on you, shyster."

Steve was getting a headache from just listening to all this banter, almost forgetting the buzz he had, which he kept to himself. He again fell asleep in the car on the way home with Al complaining to him that he had it from coke before and from booze tonight. Steve just nodded, but he knew for about a minute in the restroom he felt like he had never felt before and that he would be making a phone call sometime soon.

CHAPTER TEN

E ven before Manuel closed on the house, he knew trouble was brewing on the North Shore. Before he died, Hector Astasia had made inroads with some local pushers to supply the high school and university kids, but things had gone awry. Missed deliveries, slimmer profits to Carlos and the cartel and then one of the pushers who knew Manuel called him up to complain his customers were claiming the coke was half baking powder or sugar or something else. This was an old trick, adding sucrose or cheaper drugs like lidocaine, benzocaine or even quinine to the product, which was never more than twenty-five percent pure, anyway. But it never got brazen enough for customers to refuse to pay for it, which was now happening. So now someone or some group was obtaining and short weighting the product, distributing less but taking in more, then probably selling it to other customers-their own. It could not be allowed to continue.

Manuel and the Rendon family knew who was at the bottom of it all, it had to be the Delgado brothers, Mexicans who were local pushers for the Rendons and who were working out of a food mart in a strip shopping center in a suburb just north of Chicago where Manuel just happened to now live. The three Delgado brothers were led by the oldest, Jesus, who had bushy, unkempt hair and a thick but crooked moustache with small eyes that constantly squinted. He usually wore a dirty t-shirt and faded jeans and was totally unassuming for someone who easily made two thousand a week in cash.

The two younger brothers, Emilio and Juan, were almost clones of their older brother except they dressed better, always with pressed white shirts which accentuated their deep brown skin. Manuel called them "the waiters" because that's the way they looked.

Manuel was to meet them in the back of their store for a council, to see where things were at. He had communicated with them many times already by the pay phone near the end of the strip center where the store was, but both sides knew it was only a matter of time before a personal meeting was in order. The Delgados would already be pissed off because neither Carlos nor Antonio Rendon would be there, showing a lack of respect, which is exactly what the Rendons wanted to convey.

The meeting, however, was quite cordial, lasting only minutes, with Emilio speaking for the brothers to show *their* lack of respect, but with promises to put things right and crack down on the low-level dealers and pushers who they controlled. As a peace offering Emilio offered Manuel a case of vintage wine for the family and an engraved derringer in a velvet box for Carlos Rendon since he knew his passion for firearms.

After the meeting, things would run better for about a fortnight and deliveries were made on time with the right profits showing up and no complaints from pushers or users. Manuel had moved into his suburban house, which caused a feeling of calm to embrace him. For the first time in a long while, he seemed at peace with himself and those around him. Neighbors had come by to wish him well and he said he was a furniture salesman on the near north side naming a cousin's actual store who was told to say he worked there but was out if anyone ever called the store's number to speak to him. He came off as a fine, upstanding citizen, something he almost really wanted to believe.

This was shattered one night with a call from Antonio Rendon. No one ever called anyone at home unless it was extremely urgent, and even then, they kept conversations very brief.

"Manny, there's a big problem in your barrio. Call us back pronto from the usual place."

Manuel was half dressed, and he grumbled as he threw on a pullover sweater and some socks and looked around his bedroom for a pair of shoes. "Shit!" he thought, "Everything seemed to be going so well, even if for a little while. What's happened now?" He continued cursing as he drove to a phone booth at the Howard Street CTA train station and called back. Carlos answered this time.

"Manny, I'm sitting here with one of the pushers in your area, a waiter named Rico at a Skokie restaurant. You know him?" There were faint background noises from patrons at Club Maravel where Carlos was at.

"Yeah, I think Hector introduced me to him once," Manuel replied, knowing this can't lead to anything good.

"He tells us that Jesus Delgado and his brothers are leaning on all the pushers and runners to collect an extra ten percent from their customers above what they charge and that this has been going on for months." Manuel started to ask a question, but Carlos continued, "and the short weighting shit is still going on he says, right in their fucking grocery store at night and at some warehouse on Howard Street about four blocks from where you now live."

The implication of all this was not lost on Manuel. Yes, he had been up there for only a short time, but it *was* his territory now. "How did this guy find you, Carlos?"

"He said Hector told him all this before he died. Said Hector knew he had betrayed us but was in too deep by then with the Delgados. Told the kid that if anything happened to him, he should call me and tell what he knows."

"Carlos, this could be a set up," Manuel almost whispered, as some late-night commuters walked by the phone booth.

"Who would he set us up for, Manny? It don't make sense."

"I don't know Carlos, the Crescents, mob guys. Who knows, maybe he's a narc."

"No, I don't think so. We checked him out, and he's clean. Plus, I think it's time we put things in motion to either get them in line or end our arrangement with them once and for all." There was silence on the phone for a few seconds, then Carlos resumed. "I'm still thinking how to handle this, and I want to sleep on it. Be at my place tomorrow at noon. We'll know what's up by then."

Manuel's world seemed to collapse. A drug war. That's what was coming. And he would be right in the eye of the storm. This was his turf now and his ultimate responsibility, for better or worse. Thoughts of easing out of the trade and leading that normal life were now dashed as he stared into the darkness, driving back to the house.

The meeting at Carlos' apartment was brief and methodical. It was decided to put a scare into the Delgados rather than declare an all-out war. This would be accomplished by fire-bombing the grocery store, sending a message that we know what you're up to and straighten this out or next time it will be worse, far worse. Meanwhile, they would pinpoint where the supposed Howard Street warehouse was located. They would be indirectly hurting themselves, destroying some of their own product in the bombing, but as Carlos often said, this was a cost of doing business. Also, the fire would attract enough unwanted attention. Bodily harm would just attract more.

This would take place the following evening, Wednesday,

at two a.m. Three men would do the deed in a stolen car. Manuel, Antonio, and Ramon Santos, a half-crazed family member by marriage who loved violence and had been with Antonio when they killed Hector. They would use Coke bottles filled with gas, benzine or motor oil and old rags at the top. The bottles had been bought from an old pop machine in southern Illinois some time back for just such an occasion since they would be almost impossible to trace. Manual would drive but the car would stop, and they would all get out and each hurl two bottles at about a ten-foot distance through the wide plate-glass windows.

Even though there would be little or no traffic at that hour, the store was on a main street and things would have to happen quickly. All of them would be armed. Manuel had a snub nose thirty-eight revolver he kept only for dangerous situations like this while the other two carried Uzis, their prior guns being disposed of after Hector's death. Antonio had to rid himself of his prized pearl handle .45 caliber semi-automatic from that incident, which he didn't think about at the time. Ramon had levelled the shot gun at Hector, which had been taken apart and put in four different dumpsters in alleys throughout Chicago.

Manuel had left Carlos' apartment with a lump in his throat, one that would continue into the following night and beyond. He had been involved in gunplay before, even going to jail for attempted manslaughter some years back when three young wannabe gang members had jumped him on a run out to Aurora on the west side of the city. There had been a traffic detour on the Eisenhower Expressway, forcing him off to a side street with one of Carlos' cousins, Roberto, with him.

The kids came out of nowhere with their backwards White Sox caps yelling and waving pistols, demanding that they get out of the car. It was probably just a robbery attempt; they couldn't have known what they were carrying in their rocker panels and in the spare tire well. But what if they stole the car too? Manuel and Roberto looked at each other, drew their pieces, swung their doors open, and began firing away. They killed one and wounded another badly in the chest, the third scurrying away into some alley.

Manuel and Roberto were later identified and arrested. One of Carlos' lawyers met them in jail and told them to plead self-defense. The goods had been delivered by then, so it was simply a shootout between possible rival gangs, or an attempted robbery just gone bad. Since both their records were clean, at least as far as felonies were concerned, they did minor time for attempted manslaughter. The lawyer had somehow greased the wheels. But the incident still haunted Manuel, even if suppressed by the passage of time. Now there could be another one to start the cycle all over again.

He spent the next day trying to be as normal as possible. Making some collections, following up on new possible exchange sites with one of Delgado's people (but refusing lunch with him due to his stomach issues) and having a noise coming from his fan belt on the Benz checked with a mechanic he knew were all part of the day.

He ate a very light supper, some left overs from a fast-food joint, and waited. He drifted off to sleep and awoke about eleven thirty. They were coming by for him at one forty-five; he would walk to the corner of a main street and wait to be picked up. Antonio and Ramon were right on time in a 77' four door Impala, freshly removed from the streets of Chicago during the last hour or so. Antonio scooted over so Manuel could drive. There was a light blowing snow in the air that swirled around the car as they drove, otherwise everything was still.

"You ready Manny?" Antonio smiled. He had done this many times and truly seemed to enjoy his work.

Manuel nodded. Antonio put his hand on his shoulder as he turned his head back to talk to Ramon in the back seat. "Manny used to be a star pitcher as a kid. That's why he's here tonight. He's our ace, our best shot, eh Manny?"

"That was a long time ago when my arm and my eyes were good, a time when I could pitch in a vacant lot and only your brother could hit off of me."

"Yeah, but these are huge fuckin' plate-glass windows you could hit blind," laughed Antonio. Because he laughed, Ramon did as well.

They drove on. The streets were almost too quiet, no cars, no people, just a flagpole clanging in the distance up ahead from the wind and the snow coming down heavier. The strip center had a small parking lot that ran across the front, vacant except for a pizza delivery van from one of the stores. They stopped in front of the food mart, a corner store at the end of the strip center with its two large plate-glass windows separated by a single glass door. This was not like certain parts of the city where iron bars covered every opening. The windows were covered with paper signs visible on the outside, mostly hand lettered, lettuce for sale, twenty-nine cents a head, cucumbers, etc.

With the engine running, Antonio took out a silver lighter and they emerged from the car, quickly lighting the six bottles, waiting for a minute for the flames to burn down the rags to the bottle necks. Then each one quickly threw the bottles, not extremely fast for the wind to possibly blow out the flames, but hard enough from about ten feet away to break the glass. They waited for the flames to rise inside the store, followed by wrenching explosions from the gasoline.

They got back in the car as Manuel threw it into drive, turning to go north on the adjoining side street to avoid being seen by any cars passing by on the main boulevard. Just as they turned down the side street, two men, one in an old t-shirt and another in a long sleeve white shirt, jumped out from a back entrance of the store and started firing at the side of the car with handguns. Everyone ducked down as Manuel yelled, "It's Jesus and Emilio!" Manuel instantly realized the Delgados must have been working in the lab they had in the back of the store.

As the car sped past them, Antonio turned to Manuel and barked, "Back up!"

"Tonio, we're clear. It's done!"

"I said back up! They've fingered us!"

"Shit, fingered us, they'd know it was us, anyway!" Manuel said.

"Throw it in reverse, Manny, let's finish this," Antonio gritted his teeth as Ramon reached under the front seats and pulled out two machine pistols, handing one to Antonio.

"Okay, Tonio, but this is on you," Manuel shook his head. They pulled the safety switches off and cocked the guns.

"Damn right it is."

Manuel threw the car in reverse as it buckled until they were about fifteen feet away from the Delgados while the windows went down, and Antonio and Ramon opened fire from the front and rear windows on the passenger side. The Uzis riddled Carlos and Emilio, who crumbled like emptied sacks on the street next to the curb as the car sped by in reverse. When it was by the front of the store, Manuel put the car in drive and as he slowly drove by, Antonio and Ramon again sprayed the bodies with bullets.

Suddenly from an alley across and perpendicular to the street on the driver's side, Juan Delgado emerged and started firing a small caliber pistol with both hands almost blindly at the car. Manuel hit the brakes as everyone ducked down, but when they heard a repeated clicking sound they peered up to see Juan yelling and cursing as he reached into his pocket to try to reload. Now Manuel reached for his snub nosed thirty-eight while he threw the gear shift into park and lowered his window and opened his door, ducking behind it. He fired several shots, two missing but one hitting his target in the thigh, causing him to collapse to the curb.

"Finish him Manny!" Antonio yelled, but as he turned to look at Antonio, Ramon swung open his door and he obliged, briefly spraying Juan until he too heard a repeated clicking indicating his magazine was finished. Lights in the homes down the block started to come on and with that the car doors slammed shut and Manuel again sped north down the side street, then weaved through more side streets until they reached an old lumber yard at a street's dead end where Ramon's Trans Am was parked. As they got out of the bullet ridden Chevy, they stuffed their weapons in a black canvas bag.

Manuel's right hand was visibly shaking as Ramon drove slowly down the dark street.

"Take it easy," Antonio assured him. "It'll be okay. We did what we had to do."

The car pulled up slowly to Manuel's house, and they let him out without anything being said. A campaign poster from the primary election startled him as it flapped in the breeze against a light pole it was taped to. "What a mess," he thought. "What an awful mess."

CHAPTER ELEVEN

Steve awoke on a Friday morning and realized he had overslept. Shit, it was nine forty and the clock radio had gone off and it was always set at the same volume, but he had slept right through it. He had bought some coke two days before from Stu, less than ten grams for fifty bucks, and had been using it the last couple of nights. It was like that first time at Stu's apartment. It was good but not great. Not like that vial Manny had given him. Not even close.

He called into work and was going to make up some excuse about his stomach. He didn't reach his boss, a senior V.P. who didn't seem to be in much lately since Mayor Byrne had appointed him to some task force on banking irregularities. But he did talk to the department secretary, which was a relief in itself. He really did have a stomach problem. It ached from hunger, an occurrence that happened frequently hours after he used the coke. When he sniffed it, the euphoria seemed to suppress his appetite for hours, but then it came back with a vengeance so that later on he didn't just eat food. He attacked it. Such was the case this morning and with nothing in the house, he figured he'd get dressed, barely, and saunter down to the diner about a block away for some breakfast.

The cold March air seemed to revive him, and he walked quickly along the old, broken sidewalk to the sounds of just a few cars on Chicago Avenue riding over the slush in the street from an overnight snowfall. Most of the people who worked were already there.

At the counter, he ordered breakfast and grabbed a section of the Trib that was left on the counter. The minor headline on the first page related the story of a Wednesday night shooting in a neighboring suburb about five miles from here that left three men dead. They were all Hispanic names and were apparently involved in the drug trade. Police thought they had found the suspects' car a few blocks away, but it had been stolen. They were not naming any suspects yet because they probably didn't have any. The article went on to state that this was the fifth shooting involving the drug trade in so many months and that police were now working closely with the new combined DEA and FBI task force that had recently been commissioned at the federal level.

After eating an omelet and finishing the paper, he reached into his wallet to pay. There, in the corner of the billfold, was Manny's card. He turned it sideways and looked at it on the back, holding it up like it was a fine jewel. He thought that he really should call him after he had the greatest high in his life. But what if he was opening up something, becoming involved with someone he knew nothing about? And those guys at the table with him? They weren't exactly PTA board members, as he chuckled to himself. Then there was the cost. Manny's blow would have to cost a lot more than Stu's. It only made pure economic sense. Caviar's more than tuna. He stuffed the card back in his wallet, this time behind some seldom used credit cards and his library card. He'd think about it.

The rest of the day, he relaxed and napped sporadically. He was supposed to call Becky and Eric's cousin, Riva, who he talked to last week for an hour. He was floored when she suggested that she had a friend who she wanted to fix him up with. He had resisted at first, but as they talked and upon reflection; he figured it couldn't hurt. He had thought it might look bad to the family and they would all not approve, but this *was* coming through family and if they were pushing for it, didn't it have to be acceptable? He was supposed to call Riva tonight. He had met Riva several times. She was a free spirit, a bit older than he was and was currently dating a dermatologist, but they were breaking up because she wanted to move to Israel.

Riva was fairly religious, and that bothered him because what if whoever she wanted to match him with was the same? He'd have to tell her that was a deal breaker. The one thing that would set him off was religion. He now believed his prayers at the hospital were not just in vain but stupid, because he hadn't prayed to anyone. There simply was no God, nothing at all existed beyond what happens here on earth. Wars, death, all of it, it's random.

He cursed people who thought otherwise. Especially the simple-minded who said no, it's not random, everything happens for a reason. He always remembered scolding his grandmother when she said that years ago as a freshman in college when over the summer the love of his life at the time, Lily Stibic, was killed by a hit-and-run driver. That time had shaken him to his core and there was no 'reason' that it happened, but he still believed in God, that people are charged to do good. But Lily wasn't sick and dying. He hadn't had a chance to pray for her.

He *had* prayed for Becky, over and over, bargaining with the Almighty that he had never prayed for much in his entire life as if he had points saved up. And it did no good. If anything, Steve Kaufman was logical and now to him religion just wasn't. Sure, he'd taken a course or two in college that tried to explain fate, the age-old situation facing the problematic rebel and all of mankind. He read the darker side, Camus, Sartre, and Franz Fannon. Through it all, he wanted to believe that it was still possible to believe in a supreme being, the slaughters and genocides notwithstanding. He tried to understand various points of view, but in reality, he had still believed in God because he *should* believe.

So now you had someone who scorned the belief that a God with all this biblical power would not interfere in the lives of mortals to keep them from doing evil things or letting bad things happen. He had gone from a belief that bordered on indifference to full faith when his wife was sick, to a vengeful atheist upon her death. He not only didn't believe, but he couldn't tolerate to be around anyone who did.

His behavior had become a bit dangerous in this regard. A week ago, on a Sunday morning when he came back to the apartment after buying a newspaper, he confronted a tall, lanky boy of about eighteen in the front hallway. He was wearing a long-sleeved white shirt which looked like he had slept in it, no jacket, and a woven head covering clipped to his hair with a bobby pin. Tucked under his arm was a thin, black folder. The head covering would have been enough to set Steve off, but to top it off, he had a blue button over his shirt pocket which said, "Jews for Jesus."

"Hi, I'm looking for Hal Gold. He's supposed to live here but I don't see his name on the doorbell list," he rapidly said through thick pop bottle glasses.

Steve eyed him suspiciously and snarled, "I've lived here for a while, and I don't know of any Hal Gold being here."

"Well, he filled out one of our cards and sent it in to us and it has this address on it so he must live here," the boy challenged, pulling an index sized card out of his folder but not showing it to Steve.

"Not unless he just moved in very recently and no one's lately moved in or out," Steve replied, now almost in the boy's face.

"I'll try tracking him down at our area headquarters. In the meantime, could you let me in? I'd like to knock on people's doors or leave some literature under the doors if no one's home."

Steve's fists were now clenched. "Look asshole, I don't know you and judging by what you're handing out, I wouldn't let you in even if I did." His eyes narrowed, and he turned rapidly towards the door to find his key, hoping that would be the end of it.

The boy remained fairly calm. "I don't see what the problem is," the boy continued, "You've got to explore new things in life, the mind is like a muscle, and you can't be closed to..."

Steve clenched his keys and wheeled around. "Look, this is private property and besides that, I personally don't believe in whatever or whomever you do, whether it's Jesus, Yahweh, Buddha, or Mao. You got that? So, get the hell out of here because I won't hesitate to call the cops for trying to trespass or maybe I'll throw your sorry ass out of here myself but first take your beanie and stuff it down your throat before I do!" Steve realized he was yelling and that his voice was trembling slightly.

The boy rapidly unzipped his folder and put his form card inside and turned towards the door muttering, "you don't have to be such a jerk about it."

Upstairs, Steve thought about the incident. Was he losing his mind, or did this kid just catch the wrong person on the wrong day? He peered out the window to see if the kid was coming back into the building, but there was no sign of him. There was a rush of adrenaline through his ears that still hadn't abated. The old fight-or-flight response and he was ready to fight. A week later, thinking about the incident still found his heart beating faster.

Later that day, he remembered he had to call Riva back who wanted to fix him up with a girl named Barbara, a biology grad student at Northwestern. If it had been humanities, philosophy, or something even close, he would have said no. Steve had promised her on a Friday night call that he would call her back, but he suddenly decided to make another call first.

He dialed the number on the card and listened to a recorded message telling him the number had been changed and stating the new number, with a 677 suburban area code from a 312 City of Chicago one. He hesitated for a minute as he hung up, wondering if he dialed right, if Manuel Cruz had moved away or if something more sinister had happened, considering the associates he had seen him with at that club. But he thought he should play this out, so he dialed again, took down the new number, hung up and dialed it, letting it ring a few times until a male voice answered, "Hola."

"Hi, is this Manny Cruz?"

"Si, who is this?"

"My name's Steve Kaufman. I met you the other week at that club in the men's room," he stammered, angry with himself that he sounded so formal, like a phone solicitor.

There was silence for a few seconds. "Yes, yeah, sure. You were feeling pretty good after my token gift. How are you doing, my friend?"

"Fine. I, I called your number but wasn't sure it was right because they said there's a new number and I wasn't sure if I should try that, but I did and..." He clearly felt like an idiot.

"No, no, it's okay. I just moved from the city up to the north burbs, probably not too far from you, just west of McCormick Boulevard."

Steve felt relieved. "Oh, that's great. Nice area. Hope you're settling in." He paused for a few seconds. Well, here goes. "Look, I was wondering if we could maybe get together and transact a little business, but it would have to be a little because I really don't have a big bankroll. I mean, if you can't, you can't. I'd understand."

"Anything you want, my friend, large or small." Manuel was clearly impressed with the fact that Steve was speaking in general terms, a smart kid since the possibility always existed that the phones were tapped. "It's best to see me at the club. I'm usually there Tuesdays, Thursdays, and sometimes Fridays. Saturday it gets nuts with the crowds. Tourists, out of towners. Why don't you come by this Tuesday or Thursday?"

"Yeah, that's fine Manny, but last time I was there, my friend used some guy named Arnie to get us in. Is that gonna work for just me?

"No, just tell them you're looking for me. You'll get in."

Steve could hear the TV in the background, which had the Nightline news show on about the Iran hostages. "You watching Nightline?" he asked.

"Yes, on and off. They have to get those guys out, but our president and his people can't seem to get anything done."

"No, they can't," Steve agreed. "The whole country's begging them to do something and it's like no one's listening." He realized maybe he was sounding too talkative and didn't want to seem overly anxious. That could affect the price of the goods and a lousy way to negotiate. So rather than rush over on Tuesday, he said, "I'll come by Thursday around eight if that's okay."

"Sure, sure. Look forward to seeing you again," and he clicked off.

Steve hung up the phone slowly. What the hell was he doing? He could be getting into something deeper than he ever imagined. What if he dealt with this guy and he found out where he worked or lived? If he ever got angry at him, he could blackmail him, or worse. There was still time to back out. All the way to Thursday. He doesn't know my phone number, probably wouldn't remember me at all with the passage of time. And yet he never felt better than after trying his magical powder and feeling good was not something that came very easily these days.

Okay, he'd think about it some more.

The second call was to Riva, who went on and on about the biology grad student and how nice but brilliant she was. Just to shut her up, he agreed to call her during the week and see if she was free for Saturday night, the whole idea being that she would be.

"Then you'll call her. It's all set."

"Okay, okay, I'll call her. During the week. She's not religious, is she?"

"No, well I don't think so, but what difference…oh, yeah, that's an area we don't want to get into."

"No, we don't."

"Well, she's a biology major, probably going to end up in medical school. So, she's well read on Darwin, I suppose, but hopefully not the Bible."

"Fine, we'll see what happens, no promises."

"Oh, perish the thought you have a good time."

"Goodbye Riva."

"Bye Steve."

The rest of the weekend dragged on, laundry and shopping. No plans for that Saturday night, although a couple of old friends from school, Rogoff and Keller, wanted to see him for drinks and darts at Biddy Mulligan's on Sheridan Road. He passed. He almost looked forward to work, which was strange. He had only a handful of new active loan files to review and write up and not much else going on except hand holding customers. There was talk about the department laying off staff, though strangely, he really didn't seem to care.

But there did seem to be an excitement in the air, particularly downtown. There was a feeling of action, of electricity, of things about to pop. As though at any moment, one's senses would be assaulted. Things were happening. John Wayne Gacy had just been convicted of who knew how many murders. Bodies were still turning up. Mayor Byrne did or said something strange every day. And the hostage situation in Iran was becoming more intense. On and on, every day it was something happening at rapid fire.

And the snow was melting. People were walking around as if it were a balmy seventy degrees with light or even no coats, a few idiots in shorts and t-shirts. It reminded him of when he was back in college in those late 60's and early 70's with the war and the protests and every day holding out something new and exciting.

When Thursday afternoon arrived, he was asked by Stu and the boys if he wanted to go to a strip club on south State Street for the last matinee, but he declined saying he had to meet someone after work and left them to wonder who and why. He grabbed dinner at a two-dollar steakhouse on Wabash and went over to the library at Roosevelt University to kill some time.

He went into the restroom there to take a whiz and look at himself in the mirror before hailing a cab over to Rush Street. He combed his wavy black hair straight back to try to look less boyish, but the bags under his hollow eyes from lack of sleep lately took care of that problem. She had always said his brown eyes jumped with enthusiasm, but now they looked like two dull brown coals against sallow skin. He had on a brown hound's tooth sports coat with a gold shirt and print tie, not typical banker attire, because he didn't want to look like some pencil necked geek tonight, like a "suit" as they were called. Becky had picked out the Alexander Julian jacket for him at Baskins. It was his favorite sports coat and it fit his still trim figure like a glove.

Rush Street was booming on a Thursday night, people readying themselves for the weekend, starting a little early. What was the old saying, 'don't buy a car built on a Friday or a Monday'? The bald black bouncer wasn't there when he rang the bell at Club Maravel. In his stead was a young Hispanic male with striking good looks, thin, with sad eyes turned down at the corners, a bit like Manuel.

"Hi, Manny sent me."

"He did, eh hombre?" The man smiled a perfect set of teeth at him. "I think I know him. He's my brother. Name's Jesus." He held out his hand as the door swung wide open.

"Steve, Steve Kaufman."

"Come on in. He's at a table over near the bar. Do you know him by sight, or should I lead you to him?"

"No, we've met. I think I can find him. Thanks."

"Sure. There's a coat room down the hall."

"Yeah, I remember it. Thanks again."

At a table near the bar as smoke was rising up and swirling in a sort of eerie way from the spotlights towards the ceiling, he could make out four people at a table, two in the middle and one at each end, none of them with their backs towards the door. Sort of like a TV family facing the camera or a famous gunslinger in a saloon. Manuel was in the middle next to a larger man with long pulled back hair who he had seen from before, along with a dapper, younger man to his left who looked white. While to Manuel's right was the beautiful long-legged beauty whom he had also remembered from his prior visit.

Steven approached the table slowly while all eyes gazed up at him. He hoped Manuel would remember and maybe introduce him, so he wouldn't feel like a total idiot. His overcoat was still on and that was a good thing, he thought, not to be presumptuous that he might appear to be staying a long time.

Relief came over him as Manuel smiled and got up. "Steven, it's you, my young friend. Come here and sit down. You look worried. Don't be, you're not intruding."

"For business, you never intrude," said the large man and the others all laughed.

Manuel held out his hand and Steve shook it firmly. "Pull up a chair from behind you."

Steve swung around to grab a chair from the table behind him and noticed a young Hispanic couple sitting there. He was about to ask if they minded when Manuel beat him to it. "It's okay, they won't mind." The couple both nodded their heads in quick agreement at the same time and Steve swung the chair around in one motion and was about to sit when he realized he hadn't been introduced to the others and was about to offer an awkward introduction when Manuel again came to the rescue.

"Steve, this is a relative and very close friend of mine, Carlos Rendon, and his brother Antonio." They both rose at the same time to shake Steve's hand. Carlos had a grip like a vice while Antonio's was also firm but very quick. "And this is their sister, Angela."

She held out her hand in a sort of wrist bent way where he didn't know whether to shake it or kiss it, but he decided on the former and she responded in kind. They both smiled at each other. She seemed a bit older than him, still in her early thirties and drop dead gorgeous. She didn't have much make-up on which she really didn't need, with a perfect dark face framed by beautiful black hair and wide brown eyes with full lips.

They all sat. Manuel commented on his sports coat. "Last time I saw you, you had on a suit, like a real banker type. Now you're more Saturday night. It looks good, sharp."

"Well, I *am* a banker so that explains the suit, but you're right. I felt like being a bit more casual today."

"You work downtown?" Carlos asked.

"I do. I'm a real estate loan officer at Columbia National Bank."

"They're really big," someone commented. The small talk continued, but it got serious when Antonio asked if he was married, and he told them the story about how he was a young widower and how that came to be. Even with all the noise in the club, it became very quiet at the table.

"Is that when you started to...experiment?" Angela asked, the first words she had spoken.

Steven looked at her. The face, eyes and lips were like nothing he had ever seen. "Yes," he said, almost in a whisper, and nodded.

Manuel tried to lighten the mood. "Well Steve, if we can make life a little easier for you, then we've all succeeded."

Steve nodded almost solemnly. What would his wife and family think if they saw him here now doing these things with these people? Then he stiffened in his seat and thought that if she was still alive, he wouldn't be here, but because she left him, he was, and that's that.

"I agree. Life is short and we should live for today," Steve said. The others nodded or muttered in agreement. Meanwhile, a waiter came by and gave everyone the same drink. Steve looked at the glasses.

"Tequila," Antonio said. "Jose Quervo. Very good." He downed his in one gulp. Steve looked at his glass, hunched his shoulders, and took a swallow.

"Nice, very smooth."

Manuel slapped his hand on the table. "Okay then. Here's

the deal. This stuff I gave you to try is very good, very pure compared to the other shit that's out there. We're how you say suppliers, so you deal with us. There's no middle man to run up the price and carve it up and water down the stuff. I like you; I told you that. I'll give you a couple of grams for one-fifty. That'll start you out and last a while, depending on how much you use at a time. This stuff is good, so you only need a milligram or so at a time, so it should last. But I'm telling you," he said as he pointed his finger at him like a scolding father, "as time goes on you are going to have to use more at a time to get the same effect."

"Makes sense," Steve responded. "Do we do this now, here?" Out of the corner of his eye, he kept noticing that Angela had not stopped looking at him since he related the story about Becky.

"No," Carlos shook his head. "We never do any business here. It's not very wise as we have many, how would you say, prominent and substantial customers, hefes, where the initial contact was made here, but that's as far as it goes."

"Steve, you know where the self-park garage is at Randolph and Wells?" Manuel asked.

"Sure, my friends sometimes park there if they drive down to work."

"Well, there's a stairway next to the elevators on the Wells Street side. If you can be inside the stairway on the second floor at exactly four o'clock tomorrow, someone will meet you. You go up the stairway and he'll be coming down."

"I'll be there."

Carlos looked at his Rolex and nudged Manuel.

"Listen Steve, we have to be somewhere in about fifteen minutes. So, you got it straight about tomorrow?" Manuel looked at him intently.

"I do, and thanks. I appreciate it."

"No problem. You know I'd like to see you again when we have some more time. You still got my number, right?"

"Yep, got the new one on your card."

"Well, remember, you can always try to find me here Tuesdays, Thursdays and..."

"Fridays. I remember."

"You do. You're a smart guy, Steve."

The four of them started to get up, and Steve followed suit. Everyone quickly shook hands with him, and he made his way towards the front of the club, noticing that they went out of a different exit by the bar. She shot him a final look that he caught.

He hailed a cab cruising across the street to go to the train station. On the seat of the cab was a part of the Sun Times and he started to read an article in the faint light about how a crippled boy at La Rabida Children's Hospital who was given no hope of ever walking again was finally taking his first steps after six operations and endless therapy. His mother said she knew it would happen someday, that it wasn't a miracle as others had claimed, just a test from the Lord that she and her family had to pass. If they kept their faith, they knew they would come through it, and now they had.

Tests, he thought. Is that all we are is damned lab rats to be tested by something or someone all powerful? Is everyone's life a sliver of the story of Job? Fuck it, he thought as he flung the paper across the seat. Go test someone else.

CHAPTER TWELVE

The next day Steve was right on time at the garage and a young boy in a torn Georgetown jacket came bounding down the enclosed stairway stopping just long enough to hand him a package that looked like it was the Book of the Month Club selection inside a plastic bag and held his hand out while Steve pressed seven twenties and a ten into it. The object just fit into the pocket of his topcoat.

Earlier that same day before the end of work, Al had come by his desk with no one around and told him that Stuart was getting some more stuff in tomorrow from a street pusher off of North Avenue and asked Steve if he wanted any.

"No Al, I think I'll pass. The stuff's getting expensive, and I really think I should lay off of it for a bit. Hell, you remember last Friday when I overslept after doing a line the night before in the apartment. I really don't want that happening again."

"But you also said you were at a bar earlier that night. You know you can't mix the two. Shit, a seventh grader knows that."

"I know, I know. And it won't happen again. That's why I'm laying off. I like to go to bars anyway and watch the games and stuff. I know I can't do that with coke."

It was all lies, but he was friends with these guys and wanted it to stay that way, even with Jack. What was he going to say? I'm getting stuff much better than you'll ever know and for a lot less?

"Well, suit yourself. We're gonna eat first at Borelli's if you change your mind."

Steve nodded. When Al left, he pulled the package out of his bottom desk drawer, hidden under several reams of loan analysis reports, stuffed it into his briefcase, and waited for five o'clock. He briskly walked to the elevator and out of the bank building onto LaSalle Street. He wanted to stop at a drugstore on Madison near the commuter station before catching the five thirty-five express but thought it unwise given what he was carrying.

A girl passed by him going the other way from the station who looked like Angela, only not as pretty. He had to admit he was intrigued by her, especially when she turned to look at him before exiting the club. And the way her eyes had followed his every word. He was sure he was making more out of it than there was. Anyway, they were from totally different worlds, and he would probably never even see her again. But he couldn't stop thinking about her, not even so much in a sexual way, although that surely crossed his mind, but about talking to her and just getting to know her and then maybe more. This was not a dinner and a movie girl. He laughed. Hell, she could *be* in the movie and probably have him for dinner.

The train was unusually packed, even the smoking car where only the regulars braved, which meant some unaccustomed travelers there would be trying to remove the smell that would impregnate their coats and jackets for a long time to come.

After passing through that car and finally exhaling, he found a lower-level seat next to a fiftyish executive type whose head was entirely buried in the Wall Street Journal. Having nothing to read, Steve decided to doze, thinking about what he would do that evening, including opening his package and calling his blind date for Saturday para-Riva. He approached the first with far more anticipation than the second.

After eating leftovers and going through the mail, he realized he forgot to check the answering machine. His mother had called saying his cousin Roy, who lived in a small town downstate, had asked about him and would call him directly. Roy was sort of the oddball of the family, and it truly was a small town, a hamlet really, just off of I-55, about an hour or so out of Chicago called Carrol. He had come to this place due to a friend he went into business with making, of all things, stained glass windows. The partner had died, suddenly, leaving Roy with the option of selling and moving back to familiar environs or staying down there.

"A Jew in a small town, he'll never last," Uncle Bernie had said, as had the entire family.

But Roy lasted, and prospered, so to speak. He got along well with his neighbors, although having an active social life there was questionable. The thing about it was Roy was never very sociable anyway, so it really wasn't much of an adjustment. As far as business, his beautifully designed glass windows sold themselves, so he didn't need to be personable in business, either. He did have a girl he dated on and off who lived about three towns over, but he claimed it wasn't close to being serious.

Steve always liked Roy; he was older than Steve, but they had been friendly going back to when they were kids in Chicago's West Ridge neighborhood. When Becky died, Roy hadn't come in for the funeral because he felt that he didn't want to close up his shop and didn't get along well around the family, anyway. But he sent Steve a long, solicitous letter about how sorry he was, how he always liked Becky and about death and loss. Steve was more appreciative of the letter than of many other people who showed up in person. He thought about calling Roy, but decided to wait. He still had to call this Barbara girl about Saturday, deciding to do this first before trying Manuel's white treat, even though he preferred the reverse order, realizing that he could hardly call her if he was high.

Thankfully, Riva had talked to her earlier in the week, telling her Steve was very busy at work and probably wouldn't be able to talk to her until tonight, all per Steve who had no trouble lying these days.

In a brief but cordial conversation, they made arrangements to meet at her apartment before having dinner at a Chinese restaurant in downtown Evanston. She sounded pleasant enough, but kept talking about Riva, whom she knew from a job they both had last summer. This, of course, annoyed Steve and he cut her short, saying he had another call to make to someone who was ill before the guy went to bed. Then it was on to try the snort.

He poured a little bit, about the size of a dime, on the glass coffee table in the living room. Taking a quarter of a straw he had cut from the kitchen, he inhaled it with one strong sniff, leaned his head back and felt a cold rush come over him, like he'd been broadsided by an ocean wave. The colors from objects in the room seemed to converge on each other, then swirled all together on the ceiling as he looked up. This went on for a few minutes while his arms and legs began to tingle. He thought it was the hair on them and could see or imagine, although he wasn't sure, that every hair on his arms stood up straight, like blades of grass on a new spring lawn.

Once these sensations subsided, he went into the kitchen and opened the refrigerator as his mouth felt parched, as if it were stuffed with cotton. He moved some items, searching for a glass water jar he kept but couldn't find it. What he did find was a Bacardi mix that he had bought and made a few nights ago with rum. He swigged the concoction from the bottle and went back to lie down on the couch. The room seemed to be moving all around him and he could clearly hear his heart beating, a whooshing sound as he lay on one side with his ear pressed against the crushed velvet couch.

When he awoke, he looked at his watch: three twelve a.m. Shit! His clothes were drenched in sweat. He undressed and washed and brushed his teeth repeatedly as his mouth was again like a blast furnace. He set his alarm again carefully as he crawled into bed, as he couldn't afford to be late again. He fell into a deep sleep with a vivid dream of a dark Hispanic girl standing over him as he lay on a beach, laughing. She had long, dark hair and beautiful eyes. She was pointing a gun at him but kept telling him it wasn't loaded.

Friday was the perfect day to have a mostly all-day seminar put on by the HR Department about respect in the workplace as it was mercifully not interactive and most everyone in the department had nodded off in long spurts. One thing changed from the coke the night before. He wasn't ravenously hungry, just nauseous, and he ate very little at lunch or Friday night.

Saturday at six, he picked up Barbara at her apartment just north of Howard Street in Evanston. He was wearing a black jacket and a black sweater and pants. He was wearing black a lot lately, certainly not out of any mourning but out of a desire to break with the past. Even the sweatshirts and pants for weekends were black. He'd wear those to work if he could. Hell, the place was like a mortuary lately, so it fit.

She was waiting downstairs in her lobby, about five feet four, with a pretty round face and black hair in a pageboy style. Her clothes had that preppie look that was now in every make of clothing for women from Goldblatt's to Gloria Vanderbilt, the short, plaid pleated skirt with the knee socks and matching top. She seemed, well, perky.

Jesus, Steve thought. My first date and I'm going out with a brunette Doris Day. The Chinese restaurant was busy, but the hostess seated them in a small booth near the back. Steve asked if it was too noisy for her, being somewhat near the kitchen, but she didn't mind.

They talked about current events and politics, maybe to avoid other subjects. Her father had apparently been in the State Department under Ford and was now with a foundation in Washington after Carter came in. She described him as a liberal Republican and the current administration still consulted him on foreign policy. Heaven knows with the hostage crisis, they needed all the help they could find.

She had gone to New Trier High and then to NU, so they played Jewish geography for part of the time to again keep the conversation somewhat light. It then turned more serious and ultimately somber, as both knew it would.

"What was it like to be married?" she asked, batting her long eyelashes as she leaned closer to him across the table.

"Well," he sighed, "it was, as they say, a whirlwind courtship. We clicked from the moment we first met. It was just a few weeks after that when I asked her and she said, 'I do'. We were planning our one-year anniversary. One year. So are you asking, was there still the same passion and affection or…"

"I guess that's part of it," she interrupted. "I always hear the same phrases: it's give and take, you have to compromise but work on it all the time, etc., etc., and I guess it's obviously easier to do that if you're still very much in love and would do anything for your partner."

"Of course, we were still very much in love. Time tempers everything, but yes, we would have done anything for each other, although we were both pretty stubborn people who stood our ground. One thing we always promised is never to go to bed if we were mad at each other and we pretty much held to that."

"That makes sense," she agreed. "It's hard to imagine. I've

dated guys, although not that many. The relationships were sort of long term, two years, a year and a half, the last one was the shortest and that was over nine months. And you talk about things, the future, what you want out of life and all. But you seem so much more mature than those guys when I think about it, because you were married awhile and then recently went through so much." She gulped as she said this.

"You do what you have to do," he half shrugged. "I never want to go through it again. No one should have to, especially at our ages."

She nodded and put her chin on her hands, which were positioned one over the other on the table. "What is it they say, though, better to have loved and lost than never to have loved at all?"

He smiled wryly. "No, better to have loved and keep loving and don't lose it at all."

They both smiled for a few seconds as the waiter brought their food. He felt he was being rather quiet, not initiating conversations but just responding to them. He did a double take for a second as a Hispanic couple were at the register to pay and he thought the girl looked a lot like Angela, but of course it wasn't. Maybe you just always want what you can't have. He was going to mention that despite the past, he was ready to move on, ready for that next chapter. But he was unsure how to put it. It probably would be reassuring to her if she was interested in him and had major questions about what baggage he was carrying. So, for now, at least, he let it pass.

The weather had warmed to the 40's, a veritable heat wave for the Chicago area in mid-March. They walked down to a small café for coffee and pieces of cheesecake. He held her loosely at the waist as they walked.

"What does the future hold for you, Steven Kaufman?" she suddenly asked.

"Oh, hell, I still have trouble thinking past the next day or two lately. I don't know, I may start law school at night. I was talking about it with my wife a little while back."

He didn't want to wait for a response from her to this, so he shot back the same question to her. "What about you after the master's in biology? Research, med school, or what?"

"Could be either one. Med school's a long, tough grind, but I think it's worth it."

"That it is. I guess you have to want it bad enough like anything else."

"No," she looked at him hard. "You have to want it bad enough, but a lot of times that isn't enough. You have to have the smarts to go along with it and a lot of luck on the MCAT and other things. I know so many people who would make great doctors, but they'll never get the chance. I feel very fortunate to even be considered for the opportunity if that's the direction I want."

He simply nodded. He had obviously struck a nerve. They entered the small café and sat by the window at an ice cream table, and he noticed that she was really very pretty. The Chinese restaurant had been dark.

"Law school's neat," she went on. "But don't you think there are too many lawyers out there now? I mean, everyone trying to chase the dollars?"

"That could be, but I'm not just looking at it that way. I sort of miss school, just learning new things. I pretty much know everything I have to for my job, and I hear the in-house lawyers talking at work, and it's fascinating to me."

"But you want to keep your job, right?"

"Sure, I like it for now and I really can't afford to go full-time days to school. Even with loans and all. And, uh, I still have some medical bills to pay off." He looked away from her and sniffed for a second.

She grabbed his wrist. "Oh, I am so sorry."

"It's okay, it is what it is, as my grandma used to say. I'd start at night and see what happens."

He took her home, and she asked him if he wanted to come up to see the end of Saturday Night Live, as they had talked about the show a bit during dinner. He said he'd pass. He was kind of tired and hadn't been sleeping well. She nodded, seemed a bit hurt.

"Would you like to see me again?" he said, trying to make up for it.

"Yes, that would be nice. I had fun. You're a nice guy."

He kissed her on the cheek, more than a peck, but not exactly like a French officer pinning the Croix De Guerre on a hero. "I'll call you. I know guys say that, but I'm good for it."

"Okay. But do it before my finals come up."

"When are they?"

"Early May."

"Ha ha."

He went home and thought this was all too soon, but he liked her and he'd see. He took out a small plastic bag from the closet shelf behind some scarves and hats and spread a bit of powder on the coffee table for the rest of the night's enjoyment.

CHAPTER THIRTEEN

Manuel left the bar on Milwaukee Avenue at about eight o'clock that night in late March after meeting with Antonio Rendon, Ramon Santos, and two new recruits who were family, just up from the south, known simply as the Rojos brothers. They were going to help Manuel run operations in the northern burbs after the Delgados left a vacuum. It was the first time Antonio, Ramon, and Manuel had been together since the night of the firebombing and resulting shootings.

The wind whipped around Manuel's leather coat, which was unbuttoned and chilled him to the point where he shivered suddenly. He hated this Chicago weather, always had. But he was more concerned about what was happening on the streets since the shootings. Another cocaine related shooting with the Latin Crescents and a local pusher on Division Street two nights ago left two more participants dead and seriously wounded a bystander. The public outcry that seemed to be growing every day in the press, from the politicians and on the streets to have law enforcement stop the trafficking and the violence that went with it.

The new combined FBI/DEA task force had linked up with a so far ineffective Chicago Police Department's Narcotics Unit. They were making dozens of arrests, even if many of them wouldn't stick. Worse than that, they were tailing suspected dealers and pushers and there was talk about sting operations in the works. All this while Manuel was trying to rebuild the shattered family ring in the north of the city. He knew no matter how much help the cartel was giving him, the only one he could trust and rely on was himself.

As he drove north up Western Avenue and turned west on Peterson on the way to his house, he noticed a black sedan which seemed to be following him. It looked like an unmarked police car, but they usually have two occupants while this car had only one. He turned north again on a side street and pulled over by the curb, waiting to see what would follow, thinking that was a stupid move because it was probably a good spot to be capped if that was the follower's intent. He hadn't obtained another gun since the shooting and was rather helpless if something was coming down.

The driver slowed up and Manuel could see him look in his direction from his rear-view mirror, but then he kept going straight past him. He could feel his heart beating through his coat, sweater and shirt, and adrenalin filled his ears with a high-pitched ring. He took a deep breath, noticed as he moved that his back was soaking wet and pulled out to continue down the one-way side street until he came to the next main street which he proceeded to take, going no faster than about thirty, although the streets were clear and dry. He thought of how much longer this was going to continue and saw no end in sight.

He stopped at a phone booth near the house next to a gas station and called Carlos.

"I'm sure I was just followed after I left the bar," he said in a low, shaky voice.

"Don't worry about it. I've been followed now for about a week," Carlos replied in a matter-of-fact tone.

"Cops?"

"Probably so, though we don't know if they're federal or

local hombres."

"What do we do?"

"What can we do Manny? We go about our business but try to stay low. No more meetings for a while, especially at the club."

"Okay," he sighed, "talk to you tomorrow."

"Wait a second, things go okay tonight?"

"Yeah, but this is an awfully big nut for these Rojos brothers to crack. They're green."

"I know, but they're loyal and you'll ride 'em."

"Okay, tomorrow then."

When he got home, he looked around his house as he pulled into the driveway. All seemed quiet, nothing suspicious. As he unlocked the door, the thought flashed before him that maybe someone was inside. But there was total silence and things seemed the way he left them that morning. Still, just before going to bed, he peered out the curtains in the living room for the fifth time and the kitchen door in back and then picked up the phone for the third time to see if he heard the telltale clicking of a possible wiretap.

CHAPTER FOURTEEN

At work on Tuesday, the talk at lunch was about the NCAA tourney and Amanda Bilstein, a new loan trainee who started the day before.

"She must have had some connection to get the job in this loan market," Stu said.

"Have you seen her?" replied Al. "She didn't need any connection. She's just hot! That tight sweater leaves little to the imagination. She's gotta be a triple D with a twenty-six-inch waist. God, I'm in love."

"Pipe down, dickhead," Stu retorted. "She could be right out of high school and if you did anything with her, it would probably be statutory rape."

"I will say that age notwithstanding, she's quite nubile and someone here will snatch her up quickly, no pun intended," added Jack.

Everyone looked at him as if to ask what planet he was from, but that was Jack. Mr. WASP.

"Have you seen her, Steve?" Al asked.

Steve was daydreaming, as he often did lately. "Huh? No, I don't think so. Where's her desk at?"

Laughter erupted as Al cocked his head about three inches

from his face. "She sits two desks down from you. Cheez, are you a space cadet lately."

"Oh, I think I saw her talking to Rector yesterday," he replied.

"Hell, Rector probably doesn't even know what those are under her sweater," Stu smiled.

They all laughed at the mention of Rector, who was a senior V.P. in his fifties without a clue about anything going on at the bank or it seemed with life in general. When Steve thought about him, he always remembered the lines from the song Penny Lane about how little children laughed behind the banker's back because he never wore a Max.

"Oh Steve, by the way," Jack said. "Russ Cremmons passed by me right before lunch and told me he wants to talk to you about something. Told me to have you stop by his office when you had a chance. Knows we have lunch together.

"Screw up another loan, Kaufman?" asked Al sarcastically, sounding like the playground smart ass.

"Kiss off, Al. I haven't had a loan file go through in so long, there's nothing that could be screwed up."

"Well, like I said, he's obviously in today, although he sure keeps his door closed a lot," Stu said rather seriously. "And remember what I saw when he thought his door was closed?"

"But it couldn't have anything to do with that, could it? I mean, he doesn't know what we know, and he doesn't know what we do after hours," Steve shook his head. The others were all silent.

Steve stopped back at his desk to look through some old files that might have a legal problem, but this seemed very odd. Usually, he would hear about a legal problem from someone in his own department, then there might be a briefing with a lawyer in the law department. That had only happened once when he first started, and he only worked on the file for someone senior to him. For the second in command of the law department to see him out of the blue just didn't make any sense.

He decided to call up to Cremmons first. This way, he could look at the file and get a jump on things before going upstairs. After reaching his secretary, Cremmons immediately picked up the phone. "Steven Kaufman, how are you?"

"Fine Mr. Cremmons. Stu Fine said you wanted to see me."

"I did. When you have a second, can you come on up this afternoon?"

"Is there a file I should bring with or any documents?"

"No, not necessary. I'll explain when you get here." He then abruptly hung up.

Now Steve was really spooked. Maybe it wasn't about a loan at all. Maybe he did something that merited a warning before being fired or something. But what? His attendance was a bit spotty lately, but that wouldn't be an issue for the law department to handle.

No, something strange was going on. Had someone seen him with the package of coke? He looked at his desk, the picture of Becky, a few paperweights from some big loans he had closed, his pen and pencil set his folks had bought him. On his credenza behind his desk, a few scattered papers and a couple of mugs from a bank outing. Would he be packing these things up in half an hour? He had to make two calls from customers who had called earlier and started to dial the first one, if only to take his mind off the situation. He felt as if there was a band across his chest which seemed to tighten with every breath. After quickly answering the first call regarding an easy tax escrow question from a nervous customer, he could take no more, scurrying to the elevator up to the law department.

The law department had an entire floor in the bank and seemed to be constructed from an entire forest of oak trees with incredibly thick carpeting under foot. Inlaid wood paneling in halls and offices, huge desks, floor to ceiling credenzas, and bookcases were the order of the day. After nodding to the receptionist, he found Cremmons' secretary, a rather large woman in her late forties with a round cherubic face capped with her hair in a bun who saw him and simply said, "I think you can go right in, just knock first."

He knocked on the door, was told to come in and entered a cavernous office with paintings depicting the Revolutionary War on one wall, a large bookcase on another and enormous windows covered on the sides with what appeared to be velvet drapes to his left. Behind him, which he didn't see, was a built-in wet bar and shelves of Indian pottery flanking the door. Cremmons sat behind a huge, burled walnut desk in an overstuffed leather chair, a smallish, bespectacled man with thinning hair, red suspenders, and a bow tie to match.

"Mr. Kaufman, please close the door and sit down," as he motioned him to one of two wingback leather side chairs in front of his desk. Cremmons could see Steve's hands clasped nervously on the arms of the chair as he sat. "Calm down Mr. Kaufman, nothing's wrong." He leaned towards Steve, folded his hands on his desk and began. "This has nothing to do with the bank or our work here, and I must ask you to keep this in the strictest confidence. That is, this conversation we are about to have never took place. Are we clear on that?"

"Yes, quite." Steve swallowed hard. What the hell did he want?

"Do you know a man named Manuel Cruz?"

Steve's mouth dropped and his grip tightened further on the chair. He couldn't have dreamed a scenario like this, even while high on coke, "Well...we've talked and I've, I've met him a couple of," clearing his throat, "times." How the hell did he know about this? Wait, didn't Stu say he saw Cremmons doing lines on his desk one time? Shit. Cremmons is in with these guys or something.

"Yes, I'm sure you have. Mr. Cruz is, how might you say it, a business associate of mine. We are indirectly connected with an organization outside of the bank. He has, however, decided to greatly curtail his business operations in this area for various reasons and he wanted me to explain this to you...personally."

Steve's head was still swimming, in a dreamlike state. "I don't quite understand. I've only engaged in one, er, transaction with Mr. Cruz and I really didn't even contemplate any further ones."

"No matter. He still wanted me to see you personally, to express his thoughts to you regarding his business. Would you mind that?"

"No, I guess not. Should I call him or..."

"That won't be necessary. The number you have for him is probably no longer one where he wants to or can be reached. That's why I'm involved, to tell you he valued your association but that it unfortunately has to end."

"Okay, I guess."

"Good." Cremmons put down the gold Cross pen he had started fiddling with and stood up, Steve following suit. Cremmons walked him to the door, putting his arm on his shoulder. "Don't worry, everything will be fine. He may still call you to say goodbye and that the pleasure was all his. You should be flattered, not nervous."

"If you say so, Mr. Cremmons."

"I do Mr. Kaufman, I do."

CHAPTER FIFTEEN

The last few days had not been kind to Manuel Cruz. There had been drug busts with the couriers on the Aurora run and on the south side. This was not his responsibility, but it certainly affected his overall profits as a member of the inner circle.

Then it happened in his territory. Two couriers, posing as painters in an old beat-up station wagon, were busted on the way to see the Rojos brothers, now two new dealers up north, with their delivery. Almost twenty pounds of smack, street value of about half a million, had been seized in a routine traffic stop.

Manuel received a pre-arranged call from the Rojos brothers at about one o'clock the day after the bust from a phone booth outside a drug store on Dempster and Skokie Boulevard in Skokie. Things seemed to be running smoothly for the past few weeks until all this happened, deliveries were being made on time and payments were not coming up short.

Everyone, however, still felt they were being followed, from the mules coming in from planes out of Miami or crossing the border in Laredo, to the couriers up here, to the pushers and street dealers, to the top figures in the cartel. Manuel was constantly looking over his shoulder and peering out of windows and around corners, especially when on the phone.

The one Rojos brother, Alberto, was agitated and wanted Manuel to come over to their apartment right away because the two street couriers who were busted had to bail themselves out as the cartel's attorney never showed up. Now they wanted to complain in person to both Rojos brothers.

"What do they want?" Manuel asked. "The lawyer couldn't show up, but someone would have come to make bail for them. We'll get them their bail money back and the charges knocked down to possession when it's time for court."

"Yeah, but you don't understand. One of these guys is a second time felon. He had to plead for bail, and it was thirty g's in cash for him to walk," Alberto said.

"So, he wants his bail money back. You know he'll get it."

"It's more than that. He's pissed. Both of them are. We need to calm them down and make nice, that's all. Mules are hard to find right now. Everyone knows about the fuckin' task force. We gotta show them that they're muy importante to the operation. I'll have them stay here til you show up."

"Let me just grab something to eat and I'll be right there."

Alberto hung up the phone without a reply. Manuel guessed he'd have to calm him down as well. He spied a hot dog place down the street and stopped in, leaving his car by the drug store. After wolfing down a hot dog and fries, he walked back to the car, almost certain that a man was standing in front of it but disappeared as he came closer.

Manuel drove west down Dempster, traffic being very heavy. The Rojos brothers lived in a small apartment building in unincorporated Niles, way west of where he was coming from. He'd be charming, telling the couriers he'd get back their bail money and that everything would be taken care of before the trial, that they would probably be on probation, but no one was doing any time, that the lawyer screwed up and didn't make it there on time, but it could all be fixed. They'd piss and moan but ultimately go along. Sure, there were risks, but after all, where were they going to make this kind of money? Unless they were being recruited by someone else, which was always a possibility lately.

About half a mile away from the apartment, he thought he was being tailed by another black sedan, so he slowed up and let the driver pass. He looked like a cop, a younger bald guy in a suit and tie, but he sped past him and didn't seem to notice Manuel as he went by. Manuel thought of what Carlos said one time: "It's not when you think something's coming that it comes, it's when you think everything is calm and okay, that's when it hits you."

When Manuel tried to turn north off of Dempster onto the street where the apartment building was, he was met by a police barricade of two squad cars blocking the street and three officers waving drivers away to turn around. Manuel yelled out the window asking what was going on and the officers, almost in unison, said there was a crime scene down the block. He thought he saw an ambulance and at least three more police squads in front of an apartment building which looked exactly like where the Rojos brothers lived, a gray awning over the entrance as he had been told to look for. He could feel his heart racing in his chest and the back of his neck getting damp.

As he made a u turn on the side street to get back on Dempster, the worst fears crossed his mind. He took the next street north, turned east, and found a parking space near the corner of the street where the building was. He could see the police there as well. He bolted from the car and started to walk briskly, then ran towards a crowd of people milling about the scene. As he looked through the crowd that was gathering, held back by at least half a dozen officers, he saw a stretcher with a body on it covered tightly with a gray cover being hoisted on a gurney into the waiting ambulance. He asked a small man standing next to him who appeared to be Indian or Pakistani what was going on.

"Two men," he held up two fingers, "shot dead in the apartment there. Blood everywhere." He pointed to the building with the gray awning.

Manuel didn't have to look any further, and he turned around and walked away. Thank heaven he had been hungry.

CHAPTER SIXTEEN

Steven's phone rang that Saturday morning at about ten. "Steve, did I wake you?"

"No, who is this?" he muttered, lying sideways, looking at the clock.

"It's Manny. Sounds like I woke you. Sorry. Did Mr. C talk to you and tell you I'd call?"

"Yeah, he did, earlier this week." He rubbed his eyes, remembering what he did just last night.

"I know Mr. C said I'd call you, but I'd like to see you for just a few minutes sometime very soon to explain things.

The edict had come down from Carlos to those who were directly under him to sever ties with anyone not in the family or directly working for it, as the security risks were now becoming just too great. Steve obviously fell into that category. It was just that Manuel had a fondness for Steve and wanted him to know there were no hard feelings, that it was just business. Sure, it would have just been smarter to not give him a new phone number and forget the whole thing that way. Instead, however, he had notified Cremmons (who was also going to be cut off soon) and wanted to meet with Steve again, which was risky in and of itself.

"Will it be at the usual place?" he asked?

Smart boy. Manuel thought. No names. "No, there's a restaurant on Milwaukee Avenue which has a lounge. Here, write down the address."

"No, it's okay, I'll remember it."

"You sure?"

"Yeah, go ahead."

"It's 2320 North Milwaukee. It's called Ziggy's."

Steve scribbled it down on the back of an envelope, anyway.

"When should I come by?"

"Are you busy tomorrow afternoon, about three? I go to church earlier."

"Fine, I'll see you then."

"Good."

Steve liked Manuel, but he was worried. Cremmons said they will be cutting ties with him, but would they also be cutting his throat? Did he know too much? He was more than a bit worried. He was really scared.

The next morning after picking up a lox and bagel sandwich and bringing it back to the apartment, Steve decided that maybe, just maybe, he should leave a note as to where he was going with Manuel's name and last phone number along with the address on Milwaukee Avenue. Sure, they could kill him and ransack the apartment before anybody knew anything, find it and destroy it, but at least it was something. Maybe he could leave a second note in their storage space in the basement. No one would look there, where in the back in a piece of American Tourister luggage was $30,000 from a robbery he was involved with many years ago, something even Becky never knew about. Then he thought that was overkill, that he was being paranoid.

He threw on black jeans with a sweater to match after reading the paper and eating a light breakfast. His stomach had been churning all morning but stopped when he got into some tournament basketball on TV. He wanted to do another line to continue a high from last night, but thought better of it with the meeting at three o'clock. So, he set his alarm and fell asleep, something he would never do before on a Sunday afternoon. He woke up at a quarter to two and scrambled to comb his hair, wash up, and leave.

As he drove down into the city along the lake, he thought about moving into Lincoln Park or someplace closer to his job. The cost used to be a factor, but he didn't seem to care about that now. They had started a savings fund for a child's college education, not much, but now no longer necessary. He could even buy a place and use it for a down payment, along with the thirty thousand in cash, although the mortgage rates were a killer now, even at his own bank. There was obviously a lot more action in the city, but that was something he couldn't care less about right now. It was just that it was closer to work and probably a good investment.

Ziggy's was a corner restaurant and bar with a half-lit neon sign outside and dark windows. Steve entered and immediately heard noises from the bar where another tournament basketball game was blaring from the TVs. There were padded leather booths and tables which were half occupied, some people talking and some watching the game. The smell of smoke and beer filled the air. It was definitely not Rush Street.

Manuel was sitting with Carlos and Antonio in a corner booth, all of them huddled in what appeared to be a serious conversation. He spotted Steve first and motioned him over.

"Steve, compadre, over here."

When Steve saw the three, he was surprised and worried.

Only Manuel was slightly smiling. Antonio and Carlos shook hands with him first, Antonio pulling up a chair for him on the open side of the booth. Then Manuel shook hands with him, grasping his arm with his other hand. "You find it, okay?"

"Sure, no problem."

Manuel began right away. He told him how he really liked him and all, but as Cremmons had said, things were becoming very complicated. It would be best if they just parted company.

Steve actually looked crushed, like a jilted suitor and managed a simple "I understand, and I'll do as you ask."

Then Carlos spoke. "Look kid, you're three times seven. You probably know what we do for a living and everything. Right now, that's about all you know. What Manny is trying to say is, it's better off if we keep it that way, for everyone's sake."

"Yeah, sure." He paused and sighed, thinking if he should continue. "I will say I'm gonna miss what you have. I'm sort of a novice at this but I gotta tell you, it's the best I've ever had, and I've done some comparison shopping," he lied.

"Tell you what, Steve," Manuel said. "In a little while, when things cool down, someone will contact you and see if we can get you more. It won't be tomorrow or the next day, but you will receive a call."

"That would be great, Manny, and I appreciate it. I know you don't have to do this."

Antonio noticed that Steve's nose was bleeding and pointed it out to him. Steve excused himself and asked where the restroom was. He had remembered blowing his nose in the car and feeling something weird. He entered the restroom, which looked like it had last been cleaned about five years ago and ran some cold water and cleaned out the bloody nostril, then pinched it tight to put pressure on it as his mother and doctor father had taught him years ago.

After a few minutes it seemed to have worked and he emerged from the restroom to approach the booth just in time to overhear Carlos' gesturing with an agitated voice about there being no way to arrange shipments to the northern suburbs. "Every way we try gets fucked up. They've posed as painters, deliverymen, city workers, the narcs and feds are on to all of them, as if someone tells them of our every move. Hell, we could send the stuff by mail, and it would be safer. We've got to have a full proof way to get the blow from downtown or the north side to the near north burbs. There's a lot of green there and it's slipping through our fingers."

For some inexplicable reason, as he thought about it, Steve interrupted the conversation. "Excuse me, but there is a way to do what you want, and it's probably almost full proof," Steve blurted out, not believing he said what he just said.

"Steve, please, this is none of your concern," Manuel scolded. But Carlos raised his hand in front of Manuel to imply he should stop and turned to Steve; his interest piqued.

"What do you know of this, my friend?" he asked.

Steve gestured to ask if he should sit on the chair again, and Carlos nodded. "Look, I know what you do and I'm grateful you haven't silenced me so far, and I really don't care about your operations and all, but there *is* a way that no one will suspect someone who is a, how would you say, a courier for you to the near north suburbs." Again, Steve felt as if his words were coming out of someone else's mouth.

"And what might that be?" asked Carlos, as he crossed his arms with a doubting look.

"The train. The commuter train that I take every day up north. Thousands and thousands of business-types rush in and out every day. Say a business executive goes into the restroom at the Northwestern station on his way home from work before boarding his usual train. Another man comes in and puts a briefcase down next to him exactly like his as they stand at the sinks or even the urinals. They swap cases. I know this sounds crazy, but hear me out. Our commuter then boards his train with thousands of other commuters. When he gets off, the process is reversed. Someone else comes by and they swap cases again like before. I think it's full proof. No one would ever suspect a thing. There's a crowd of people around. It's not like the El train or airport or bus terminal or Amtrak-Union Station, where someone might suspect something like this. I'm sure people who you don't want to encounter may be watching those places, but not a commuter railroad, especially the Northwestern North Line, where the richest executives ride."

"It sounds hokey, loco, like something out of James Bond or something," Antonio said. "And why not do this on the El or subway again?"

"Again, because that's a logical place for drug trafficking to take place, even with the rush hour crowds. I would bet you, and I seldom bet, that the police or DEA or FBI or whomever, are watching the busy El or subway stops. Look, Russ Cremmons buys product from you and whoever decided to let him in, well, it's brilliant. It's the same concept: who the hell would suspect a bank executive or attorney to carry lots of drugs or cash?"

"So, Steven, Esteban," Carlos said as he started to play with a bottlecap on the table, "why shouldn't we ask Cremmons to be our courier, after all, we've known him longer than you and doesn't he take your commuter train to the north burbs like you?"

Steve pondered this for a second, then actually smiled. "You could, except he gets off at some stop in Winnetka where not that many people get off the trains. A stop for the very wealthy. If a switch was done there, someone could spot it a mile away."

"If they were looking," added Carlos.

"Right, if they were looking. But once someone sees something funny at that station, maybe all of a sudden certain people *start* looking."

"But I'll bet where you get off, someplace in Evanston is it, that's very crowded at rush hour. No one is looking," Carlos said with a wry smile, the others in the booth following his lead.

Steven then smiled. "I suppose that's true."

"Steve, would you excuse us for a minute?" Carlos asked. "Here, grab yourself a beer or something at the bar, just give us a moment," and he handed him a five-dollar bill.

"You know, maybe I shouldn't have mentioned all this. Maybe it's just crazy talk. After all, you guys are the experts and I'm just some smart ass who..."

"Steve, it's okay," Manuel said. "Like the man said, just give us a minute."

He sauntered towards the bar and caught the bartender's attention, ordering a beer. He sat at the bar, one eye on the TV, the other on the three men huddling in the booth. "Why, oh why," he thought, "did I ever bring this up?" Am I fuckin' nuts or something?" But after realizing how stupid it would be to become involved by just suggesting something like this to these men who were professional drug lords and probably killers, after thinking of the consequences if HE were to actually become involved with them, he was still amazed to rationalize to himself that it WAS an excellent plan, the perfect cover.

He thought back to 1968 in college when he and three friends had robbed a warehouse on Goose Island, partly to dare and commit the perfect crime. And so far, thirteen years later, it was. But that was a one-shot deal, and it barely came off. This would be an ongoing thing, much riskier.

Where's your mind, Kaufman?

After about ten minutes or so, which seemed like an hour, Manuel stood up and motioned him over and he left the five and his beer, walking somewhat apprehensively over to the booth as he was motioned to take the same chair. Manuel spoke while the others looked at him in serious (almost deadly) silence. "Steve, we like you. And your plan, as loco as it seems, just might work. We could recruit someone else to do what you propose, maybe even one of our own who looked Anglo enough, but there are definite advantages to have an actual businessman who's employed downtown be our commuter. You're a lawyer or..."

"A banker," he interrupted.

"A banker, better yet. And I bet YOU yourself want to try being the commuter for us, otherwise why would you have brought the whole scheme up, am I right?"

"You know, Manny, I didn't really think about it at the time. I just sort of blurted it out, but while I was over at the bar, I was thinking about it and yes, I think I could really handle this."

"Well, that's good because we not only like you, we think we can trust you. But you have to understand something. This isn't a game or a thrill, it's a business, a very serious one, a life and death one. You'd be very well paid, but you would only know a small piece of an entire operation, having contact with just two people, one at the downtown station and the other where you get off. That would be the extent of your involvement and your contacts. We do that with all the couriers. It's better for them and us that way. What you would do is give me your address and phone number and someone will pick up your briefcase tomorrow and bring it back to you in a few hours or the next day. Is it old? Do you remember where you got it?"

"Sure, about a year ago, Fields in Old Orchard."

"Good. The runs would be three times a week, without fail. You would be paid at the end of the week, in cash. It would be in the briefcase when you do the drop off. Ten G's a week to start.

You will have one number to call us and only use it in an absolute emergency, but if you get in trouble, you're on your own. We've had too many courier problems lately and we don't need any more. We will contact you at home to tell you the exact details of how it will all work, but the basic idea is you will carry an empty briefcase to the station where you get on. A switch will be made with our product in another case, probably in the restroom like you said. Then when you get off, another switch will be made to give you an empty briefcase again in Evanston at the first stop?"

"Yes, Main Street. There's a newspaper stand at the bottom of the stairs that would be a good place for the switch, but whatever you think."

"Okay, we'll check it out. Do you normally carry much in your briefcase?"

"No, I hardly ever bring work home these days. Things are slow."

"Good, so again, the first thing is to copy your present case and if we can't do that, we'll get two identical new ones. Anyone asks just say the handle, or the lock broke. And one other thing." Manuel's eyes narrowed, and he leaned in close to Steve. "Also, know this. We can stop this at any time for any reason. Are you okay with all this? What do you say?"

"You know, since my wife died, my life has been pretty empty, all the way around. I know it sounds phony, but since I met you it's been somewhat exciting again. I don't care anymore about the long-term future or what it's going to bring. I'm simply living day to day, so I don't know what I've got to lose even if I'm caught, or worse."

"Yes, that's all fine, but if you don't care, you're more likely to be careless and we don't need that," Carlos retorted.

"I can promise you that won't happen. I'm a banker, after all, and a damned good one. No one pays more attention to matters, particularly details, than I do."

Carlos looked at his two compatriots with a slight smile. "Okay then, let's try it." He held out his hand to Steve, who shook it firmly. Then the other two shook hands with him and Manuel reminded him about someone coming by tomorrow for the briefcase. "They'll call you first, so expect to hear from someone."

Steve nodded, gave Manuel his address and phone number on a cocktail napkin, and Carlos rose from the booth, the others following suit. They all walked out onto the street. Manuel put his arm around Steve's shoulder. "I hope it goes well for you, my friend. We may never see you again, as there would be no need to if things run okay."

Steve nodded as they shook hands and went their separate ways.

"Fucking unbelievable," he thought as he shook his head going back to the car.

CHAPTER SEVENTEEN

T he next evening Steve's phone rang, and a man said he would be by in fifteen minutes if Steve was home to borrow his briefcase, returning it the following evening. He was good to his word and a note inside said to wait for further instructions.

Meanwhile, at work there was again talk of layoffs in all departments since the lending business was so bad. He was considered a mid-level loan officer, but just barely, and it obviously depended on how deep the cuts would be, which, of course, no one knew or said they knew.

But Steve really didn't care about the bank that much anymore. Everyone seemed to annoy him lately and his work, as he described it to Stu and Al one day (never to Jack) was "beyond boring." And of course, he had dollar signs in his eyes from the upcoming employment opportunity that was supposed to arrive with a phone call at any time now. Of course, if he was laid off, what about going to and from the train every day? The whole scheme would make anyone consider it more insane than it already was if he kept it up.

Risking a career, reputation and possibly doing jail time or being exposed to greater danger were not things a normal person did. But that was just the problem. His life was so ordinary now, so predictable and lonely, that for once, just once, he might be able to look back and say he did something very few people have ever done, even if it was illegal.

The moral question also didn't seem to faze him. He no longer believed in a God or religion, so the divine retribution factor or faith itself wasn't an issue. Her death did that. Nor was just being moral for its own sake which, at least, he used to hold on to. It wasn't a question of believing he was amoral, either. He was just at a point in life where he cared very little anymore about anything. He thought about the shame on himself and his family if caught. This had been one major concern as he drove home from the tavern on Sunday. By the time he was home, it no longer was.

The cuts were announced that Thursday, so that issue was settled, at least for now. Envelopes were handed to those employees affected, indicating they should see their supervisors. Phil Goldberg and Jan DeWitt, two junior loan officers, were to be let go, however, the other loan officers junior to Steve were left untouched. Steve knew he'd be around now and truly anticipated the call at home, as his 'cover' would remain in place.

But it wasn't until Saturday around five when the call came. It was from Antonio who simply asked if he would like to start on Monday, then Wednesday, and Friday. Steve obliged, and Antonio asked if his briefcase had been picked up and returned, knowing it had been. He then asked what train he would be taking.

"I usually take the five thirty-five. It gets me to Main Street in Evanston around five to six and it's an express, so people come pouring out there when it stops."

"Okay, Main Street. And the washrooms, downtown, where are they?" asked Antonio.

"The ones I use are on the west side of the station off the lobby."

"And you normally board that train when?"

"About ten minutes before it leaves, at five-twenty-five."

"So, if you went to the washroom at exactly five-fifteen?"

"Yeah, that would work."

"Good. A man in a black leather jacket with short hair and rose-colored glasses will come in there and find you at exactly five-fifteen. Try to be by the last stall in the urinals and make sure your briefcase is next to you on your left for the switch."

"Got it."

"Then you get off at Main Street, right?"

"That's right."

"Where is it most crowded there so the second exchange can happen?"

"When I get off the train at the bottom of the stairs going down on the east side. There's a newsstand about twenty feet from the bottom of the stairs. People are going in twenty different directions there with some people in line for newspapers, magazines, that would be ideal. From there, I walk east on Main Street across Chicago Avenue down the one block to Hinman Street on the right. That's where I live."

"Fine. A man will approach you there at exactly...when does the train arrive?"

"Five to six. And I wear a tan coat."

There was silence as Antonio pondered this. "Okay, he will be there then. If you're a minute or two late, he will buy a paper and start reading by the newsstand. If the train is early, maybe when you come down, you do the same."

"No worries there. The train is never early."

"Bueno, good. He will have a light gray coat on and a beard. Good luck my friend, I have to go." He abruptly hung up.

Steve shook his head. He was still in a state of disbelief. He could still possibly back out, call Manuel, even the restaurant, to try to find one of them to say he'd changed his mind. Or see Cremmons during the day on Monday. Yeah, that was it. Maybe he could still reach one of them. Then again, he'd look like a coward, a hypocrite who came across as this wise ass kid who had a full proof, cocksure plan that he had devised and now he had his tail between his legs and didn't want to get involved.

Then he thought maybe he could do one run, just one, and when they called again, he could say he wanted to stop. Or better yet, he could put a note in his briefcase that was to be exchanged stating "to whom it may concern: I quit after this run." Naïve, but possibly effective enough.

The truth was, however, he wanted to try it. He wanted this brush of danger in his life, which now seemed to be going nowhere in a hurry. He thought about it on and off all that day. Two friends from college called about four o'clock, Rich Marden and Gary Sheldon. He had forgotten that they had called earlier in the week to go out to dinner and see *Kramer vs. Kramer* at the show that Saturday night. They were both coming off of long-term relationships, as was Steve, sort of. He didn't want to cancel, as he blew them off once before.

"We'll get you at six thirty," Sheldon said. "We'll honk. We can go to Meyer's Tavern and eat at the bar while we catch the b-ball tournament and if we're still sober, make the ten o'clock show. Sound okay?"

"Fine Gary, but you tell Rich it's a Saturday night and even though no dates, I won't be seen with him if he wears sweats and his old grunge Illini hat."

"He won't," Sheldon laughed. "It's not just how it looks any more, they're starting to fucking smell." They both laughed. These were the last two friends from college who weren't married, and they had always been there for each other on the rebound. When he was with them, he thought of happier times where there were no bills to pay, work to get done, few responsibilities except to study and get your ass to class on time, and no long illnesses culminating in death.

It would be good to see them again, although they were at the funeral. It had been before Becky died when they last got together, but as with everyone, he didn't count seeing people at the funeral in the equation.

He was downstairs and out the lobby door, although they honked for almost five seconds, just to be annoying. He climbed into the tight back seat of Gary's Pontiac Tempest coupe. Rich's hair was combed, and he had on a button-down shirt with slacks that matched. "See," he said. "You dicks worried for nothing, and we're only going to a bar and a show."

"Yeah, but you know Richie, you're like a little kid who has to be embarrassed into doing something," replied Gary.

"I'll bet that hat you got could walk away by itself if you let it," added Steve. They joked and laughed through most of the evening at the bar where the burgers, beers and tater tots kept coming. The conversation was about their school days and invariably they played "where are they now?" regarding everyone they could think of whom they mutually knew. Steve hadn't felt this good in a long time, certainly sometime prior to when he knew she was sick. Then a dark moment occurred, almost as if it were meant for him to hear. It involved Rich's brother, also named Steve. Rich had turned quiet all of a sudden and Gary had asked what was wrong.

"It's my kid brother who's down at Meridian." This was a relatively small liberal arts college downstate. Rich almost choked as he said it. "He was in his apartment with his roommate and one other guy, and they got busted by the police down there for snorting cocaine. Someone snitched on them. They all had less than three mils of the stuff between them, which I hear isn't very much."

He put his hand over his brow. "Fuckin kid's ruined his whole life now. School threw him out after two and a half years. He's got a record now just when jobs are real tight to begin with, and my parents are naturally going nuts. My mom took an overdose of Valium the other day. Almost killed herself. Had to have her stomach pumped. The whole family's upset. Cheez." He shook his head.

What could the other two say besides "sorry to hear it" and "tough break." Steve shuddered at the story. It was almost like a sign that he should hear about this when just a few hours before Antonio had called. Or it could just be coincidence. After all, plenty of people were trying and regularly doing coke now, and college students from good homes were certainly not immune to it.

They finished their burgers and barbeque chicken and slogged out of the bar after too many beers to count. The show was out of the question, and Sheldon drove them both home. He claimed he had a pickup basketball game in the morning at some park district gym, but he was really just tired and inebriated like the others. When Steve got home, he was even too tired to find a stash and snort any, so he simply went to bed.

He slept a good part of Sunday, but there was a queasiness in his stomach, and he knew it was from the anticipation of tomorrow, the rush hour to be exact. He looked at a picture of himself and Becky, taken at the zoo almost two years ago, and suddenly started sobbing. He felt like he was letting her down by what he was about to do, that this was against everything she ever believed in, her husband dealing with drug scum and thieves who had no morals and lived for the moment. But then he stiffened and put the picture face down and thought it served her right for leaving him. This is what I have become and now this is what I intend to do. That night he slept well with the aid of three fingers of Jack Daniels and one of her old Vicodin pills that he hadn't discarded.

CHAPTER EIGHTEEN

He only had orange juice and coffee the next morning, believing he could not keep anything else in his stomach. Hell, what would he tell the boys around lunch time? Another thing he hadn't considered. He caught the train to downtown and sat with his briefcase in front of him on his lap, on top of which he read remnants of yesterday's Sunday paper. The train was crowded as usual, no one paying attention to anyone else. This would hopefully be the same way coming home.

That morning at the bank, it was actually busy. The Fed was finally easing up on the prime and the effect had finally caught up with the bank. Two customers came in that morning, one old and one new, to talk about a capital equipment lease and a refi on a real estate loan. It was good that he was busy, he thought, as it took his mind off of other things.

Lunch was beckoning by a call from Al, although Stu was at an appointment and Jack was out sick. Steve kept telling himself to eat light, not an easy task with cafeteria food. But he endured with Jello and a side of coleslaw, with a muffin for dessert, stating that he wasn't well. The small talk at lunch seemed to go right by him, his mind obviously elsewhere. He decided to bury himself in a couple of projects after lunch to take his mind off of everything. The task at hand at the end of the day could not arrive soon enough.

He was supposed to meet the contact at five-fifteen, and he was usually done with work by almost 5:00. Fortunately, no one wanted to see him at the last minute, particularly any of the senior vice presidents (which he hadn't thought about before), nor had his friends asked him to do anything after work, which he could have made an excuse for in any case.

A call did come in at about four-forty-five, but he let it ring until it went back to the switchboard while he pretended to shuffle through some papers. He checked his briefcase and emptied the few things in it, then caught an elevator to the street and walked briskly to the train, checking his watch at least every hundred yards. He didn't want to be late or early, realizing if he timed it just right, things would appear normal.

He bought a newspaper at a newsstand outside the station building on Madison Street, there being no wait as there might be if he had bought one inside. It was five-eleven, and he gripped the briefcase even tighter, even though it was almost like carrying nothing at all. After the long walk inside the building, he was in the main waiting area, which was scurrying with activity and noise. The huge depot, built in the thirties, was constructed so that if someone clapped their hands, it would reverberate from one end to the other.

He entered the washroom at exactly five-sixteen and immediately noticed a man following him in with a black leather jacket and jet-black hair, slicked back, with tinted glasses. Steve walked to the last urinal stall; a man in the adjoining stall was just zipping up and walking away. The man who had followed him then stood next to him and put down an identical case to his right, next to Steve's. Steve glanced at the man for a second and became briefly apprehensive as the man's hair was not exactly short, as Antonio had described. Yet everything else fit, so he picked up the case after a few seconds and walked to a wash basin to lightly wash his hands and look in the mirror, the briefcase being between his legs.

He noticed for the first time that day how poorly he had shaved in the morning and scolded himself. Nerves. When he glanced to the back of the restroom, the man was gone.

Steve boarded the train at his usual time, around five twenty-five. Seats were already filling up quickly for the five thirty-five express, and the prized window seats were all gone. He found a seat next to a woman who appeared to be in her early forties, frantically writing what appeared to be some sort of document on a legal pad.

The new briefcase seemed only a bit heavier than the other one, and he held it tightly on his lap while unfolding the newspaper. He opened his camel hair topcoat and began to read the paper, or at least pretend to. A thousand thoughts flashed through his mind. What if the train was late or if he couldn't find the contact or the contact couldn't find him? What if the authorities were on to the whole thing? What if some other organization knew about all this because they had someone on the inside of Carlos' group and they snatched the case, or worse, snatched it and snuffed him out? Could that happen on a crowded train or station?

He closed his eyes and tried to nap for a bit. Even though the train was overcrowded, it was amazing how little noise there was in the commuter car. Everyone was either reading or working, even those who were talking to each other did so in almost a whisper as only the click clack of the rails and occasional muffled sound from the engine horn broke the silence.

When the conductor announced Main Street as the next stop, Steve was fully awake. His heart was pounding so hard it seemed to ache. There's another scenario, he thought. I have a heart attack and they wheel me into an emergency room with my briefcase full of cocaine. He gripped the case even tighter. People started to get up and fill the aisle, himself included. His watch said five fifty-three, and the train was slowing down after its express run from the city. It was a rainy, gray day and darkness was settling in. The train stopped at five fifty-six.

The first thing he looked for as he emerged from the car was to see if anyone was there to greet him. Not the contact man, but the police, DEA, etc. His imagination was getting the better of him. Everyone walked with their heads down, scurrying left and right off the platform. Steve thought about this. People seldom looked at each other anymore, whether it was here or on the sidewalks or everywhere generally. His father had lamented about this and how society had become far less friendly than in his day growing up.

Most of the commuters descended the stairway to the street slowly, beaten down by the trials of the day, anxious to get home but moving slowly and steadily as if on auto pilot. Steve glanced again at his watch, which now showed six o'clock straight up.

As he reached the bottom of the stairs, he took two steps when a man with a gray trench coat and a gray cap approached him and thrust out a case, which Steve took and in one motion handed him his case as he walked past. The man looked almost elderly with wide glasses, a gray beard, and strands of gray and white hair peeking from his cap. That was all he could remember about him.

Steve continued to walk east on his way home, glancing over his shoulder occasionally but seeing nothing unusual. By the time he crossed Chicago Avenue across from the station and walked onto his side street, he felt a deep sigh of relief. By now, the chances were pretty good that no one had noticed the transaction. It was like an anti-apprehensive booster shot over before he even realized it. But then the wind swirled some old leaves from fall around him as if some spirits were angry. He walked quickly. A crow squawked in a tree somewhere and he was happy he didn't see it, believing if he did, it would mean bad luck.

Upon reaching his apartment, he retrieved the mail and went upstairs, opening the briefcase. It was empty except for a paperclip at the bottom of one of the pockets. This seemed easy enough, but he could still call and maybe back out if he wanted to. Maybe. He put off thinking about it as he opened the mail.

After some leftovers for dinner, the phone rang. He didn't recognize the voice.

"Everything go okay this evening?"

"Well, yes, I think so," he said, startled at the call.

"Good. You on then for Wednesday?"

"Yeeeah, I'll be there," he said, not being quite sure.

"Okay then." The caller hung up.

That was his chance if he wanted to get out and he blew it. He could still try if he wanted after Wednesday or maybe even Friday, he thought. But what would he use for an excuse? People were suspecting him at work or something? He would have to make some excuse for this Wednesday with Al and the gang as they had been getting together for dinner and to watch basketball tournament games at some restaurant/bar on Wednesdays and he did believe that this Wednesday it was supposed to be on again.

Then, for some reason his thoughts turned to how he was to be paid. This he hadn't questioned and now felt naïve about it. Cash would be in the briefcase on Fridays. What the hell was he supposed to do with ten grand in cash?

Wednesday, he simply told Al and Stu at lunch that he had not been feeling well and was going straight home. Although he was hungry, he ate a very light lunch claiming stomach problems. Both of them asserted that his malady was due to the fact that for years Becky would give him a home cooked meal at dinner and that now he was living on takeout food and leftovers, these new found habits finally catching up to him. He heartily agreed, although with all deference to the deceased, Becky had been an okay cook, not a great one, and his stomach had been just fine except for the last few days.

The Wednesday run was also smooth and uneventful. The same two men met him in the restroom and down below the station platform. Because he recognized them instantly, it all seemed less awkward. There was a note in the empty briefcase stating that they were on for Friday, unless he called a number that was scrawled on the paper. This puzzled him. Were they giving him an out? He put it out of his mind.

Friday's run was a little more hectic because he had to hustle to catch the train. Steve was just getting ready to leave but a junior loan officer seemed to be in a panic. He had some questions on a file. This was one of the things Steve had feared, although he was able to answer the stressed-out youth's questions calmly and quickly. He was maybe two minutes late to the restroom, and the man was in a urinal stall when Steve arrived. The contact put down his briefcase with a disapproving thud and grunted, then walked over to wash his hands. Steve waited a minute, then did likewise and ran to board the train.

No seats this Friday, so he stood next to a stairway of one of the double-decker commuter cars, reading a loan officer's bulletin. He ran into Chuck Shadur, a former friend from college who worked at a rival bank. They exchanged greetings and small talk. Chuck had been out of town when Becky died but had called and sent a condolence card. He asked Steve if he wanted a ride from the Main Street station, where they both got off, to Steve's apartment. His wife was picking him up and it would certainly be no bother.

This was another obstacle Steve had feared, running in to someone who might stay with him when he was going to the washroom at the station or, like now, departing the train. He had thought about it after seeing Carlos and Manuel, but would dare not bring up the issue. Steve politely declined, saying he wanted to browse at the newsstand near the train station for a while and he only lived a block and a half from the station. But Chuck could still follow him off and down the platform stairs. Fortunately, very fortunately, he said his wife always met him at the south platform while Steve and the newsstand were at the north end. Still, it was a close call and something else Steve now had to realistically consider when he weighed up the entire situation, which he planned to do over the weekend.

The transaction with the contact went smoothly and when Steve arrived home, he opened the briefcase to find a sealed envelope, licked closed and then taped by the seams. He took out a letter opener in the shape of a scimitar that his parents gave him when they were in Israel and Jordan years ago and slit the top open. Inside were one hundred Benjamins. Steve counted them, one hundred even, ten thousand dollars. He ran his fingers through the bills. They were new in wrappers. He laughed for a second, thinking they could have come from his own bank. Then he shuddered at how unbelievable this all was.

All night he paced the apartment, debating with himself as to what to do. Should he stop here? Maybe he should give the money to some charity. It was scary and gut wrenching, but the exchanges were quick and painless. If only Manuel and his cartel didn't know who he was, he could keep this a secret for all eternity, but that was stupid thinking because they did know. Like his grandmother used to say, if wishes were horses, beggars would ride. Or something like that.

In the morning, he decided to take half of the money and deposit it into his bank account, knowing that federal banking laws now required reporting of anything deposited in cash of ten thousand dollars and over. He pulled a number ten plain white envelope from out of the desk and put five thousand inside it. Then he opened a dresser drawer in the bedroom, pulled it out all the way and taped the envelope to the back of the drawer, reinserting it on its runners. He knew an uncle who did this all the time.

CHAPTER NINETEEN

He had seen a beautiful gray suit about a month ago in the window of a very exclusive men's shop on Oak Street, and decided to splurge and buy it. He would drive downtown after depositing half of the money, which he stuffed into his jean pocket. As he made the deposit at the bank, he realized that even if he deposited five thousand every week, someone may eventually take notice. He would have to rethink this part of the process, possibly opening other accounts.

It was a sunny day near the end of winter as he drove down Lake Shore Drive and turned off down Michigan Avenue. He was prepared to park in an undoubtedly expensive parking lot on Oak when he spied a metered space on the street with about twenty-five minutes left. When things go right, the world is a sunny place.

The clothing store still had the suit in the window on the end with a resplendent red tie, not too flashy but sharp, very sharp. He walked inside and an older gentleman in probably his late fifties with slicked black hair asked if he could help him find something.

"That gray suit in the window on the end, do you have it in a forty-four?" The man walked to a rack by the wall with Steve in tow. His fingers went flying through a rack near a wood-paneled wall while he chattered on how Steve had very good taste if he was looking at that suit but that he might find others in that size from a collection that just came in if they didn't have a forty-four for this suit. He then found a forty-four and whisked it out in one motion, showing him everything from the fact that it was the finest wool to the lining and stitching.

Steve asked if he could browse a bit, meaning that he wanted to be left alone for now, which the salesman picked up on. He then spotted a fitting room and tried it on, coming back out by a three-sided full-length mirror. The jacket was almost a perfect fit on a perfect day: shoulders, sleeves, waist, everything. The salesman came back and beamed his approval.

The pants were fine in the waist and the rise in front but a bit long, so the salesman scurried to find the tailor, a small Filipino man who commented that they just needed to be shortened depending on how much and depending on if he wanted cuffs. He also marveled at the fit. The salesman asked if he had a tie to match the suit and Steve asked for the one in the window. The salesman rushed to get them while Steve went to change out of the suit.

As he came back out of the dressing room, the salesman said he was still checking on the tie and if he couldn't find it, he'd give him the one in the window and replace it so Steve handed the suit to the tailor and said he'd browse for a minute while the man looked. He had wandered over to the sports coat section when he felt a tap on his shoulder.

"Do you come here for your suits?" a smiling face asked him as he turned around.

"I, well, no, not really," he stammered as the woman who he had only seen twice but fantasized and dreamt about stood in front of him. The smell of her perfume he inhaled instinctively drew him closer to her.

"I'm here to pick out a tie or two for my brother," she said, as she threw her hair back, revealing long silver earrings against her smooth brown skin. He was transfixed by her face. She could have been wearing nothing at all because his gaze never left her.

"Your brother?"

"Yes, Carlos. You do know him, yes?" Her one eyebrow was raised in a questioning manner.

"Oh, yes, of course, I just didn't really know how you were…"

"I'm Angela, by the way. You thought we were an item, yes?" she laughed. "Everyone thinks that at first. But we're brother and sister. We have a large family. I have two other brothers who are better looking than Carlos, Antonio you know, then there's Luna who lives in Fort Worth. Then I have a sister, Carmen, who is much prettier than I am."

"I find that hard to believe," said Steve, "and I'm not trying to flatter you though it sounds like it." Jesus, he thought, I'm flirting with a drug lord's sister.

"You are Steven, right?"

"Yes, Steve Kaufman." Maybe Steve the dead man if this keeps up.

"Take a walk with me." It was sort of a command the way she said it and motioned to him. He forgot about his tie, paid for the suit in cash, as she did for the two ties she had, and they walked out together, onto Oak Street, side by side. Steve chuckled at the possibility their money could have come from the same source.

The conversation went from what he did (boring banker) to what she did (boring hairdresser) to families and friends. He asked about Manuel and learned he had always had a crush on her since they were kids, but because he was a first cousin, nothing could or would ever happen.

She asked about his wife and how he was coping or not

coping and what led him to do what he was doing for the Rendon family, though they both knew better than to discuss business in any detail, especially in public. They ended up in a small coffee shop around the corner from Rush Street and after more small talk and a few cups, she dropped a bomb on him.

"So let me ask you a question, Mr. Steven Kaufman, Mr. Northwestern graduate, Mr. LaSalle Street banker. Do you like me?"

His mouth dropped and he could feel his face blush. "Yeah, sure I do, but..."

"But what? Are you too good for me because you're a big banker and come from the North Shore, or is it just the opposite, am I too much to handle because you're the quiet, sophisticated type and I live for the moment from a family that's important in its own way?" A wry smile crossed her lips, and she leaned her head on her hands across the table. Her eyelids fluttered and her long brown fingers with sculpted nails and gold rings were inches from his face.

"Look Angela, sure I really like you. But there's a few how would you say it, roadblocks, to deal with. First, I think you could have any guy, Latin, White, Black, that you wanted. I don't underestimate myself, but with you I would. Second, my idea of a date, from what I remember when I was dating, which was years ago, is a quiet dinner and maybe a movie. Honestly, somehow you don't fit that profile. Third, if it got serious, yes, there are complications with family, probably both of ours, but I'm more scared of what your family would think or do, particularly Carlos, than mine."

"Oh, don't mind him," she waved her hand in the air. "He really doesn't care what I do lately. Everything is business and more business. The more money he makes it seems, the more he wants and the busier he gets. That's why I have to pick out ties for him."

She looked around for a second, tossed her hair back, and continued. "If two people like each other or more than like, you just have to let it happen and not worry about families or where you come from." She folded her arms, and he started to say something, but she cut him off. "And another thing, you think because I'm Latin that I'm from another planet or something? I like restaurants and shows just like you do. And yes, guys sometimes, well maybe more than sometimes, kind of go loco over me, but I'm interested in you, not them."

His heart was racing. Sure, he wanted to very possibly get involved with her, find out more about her, who wouldn't? But he wanted something long term. He wanted a family. The thought of dating again frankly terrified him. Maybe it was values or upbringing, but at this stage of life he was not into one-night stands or short-term relationships. Then again, could a date hurt? "Well, I'm willing to try something if you are," he finally blurted out, although kind of meekly with his chin resting on his hand gazing into her eyes.

"You don't sound very positive to me."

"Okay, I'd love to take you out and get to know you better."

"Oh Steven, what to do with you?" she squeezed his cheeks with both hands (thank goodness it was with her palms, not her nails) and although he felt embarrassed, chills ran through him as she touched him. This girl does not stand on ceremony, no sir. "How about if we go slowly?" Just the words he wanted to hear.

"That would work," he nodded, smiling, but still quivering from her touching his face.

"I live off Division in a new high rise on State Parkway." She opened her purse and took out a business card that had just her name and phone number on it. Just like Manny, he thought. "Are you free during the week after your runs?"

"Oh, you know about them?" he asked, realizing she

probably did.

"We all know. It was a bold and brilliant plan you came up with and it will save the family business in the north suburbs."

"Well, I hope not too many people know."

"Just enough Steven. Just enough."

They settled on that coming Thursday. He was to call her first to make sure it was still on. They didn't kiss when they parted, but embraced and squeezed each other's hands. He didn't know how he came across to her, but he was beginning to believe that she was the most sensual creature to ever come into his life, including his late wife, ala va shalom (may she rest in peace).

CHAPTER TWENTY

The Monday run was as smooth as the others. The pick-up man at the Evanston station was a bit late by a couple of minutes and whispered "sorry" into his ear. Steve mentioned to Stu and Al that they all ought to go out Tuesday night for dinner and catch a basketball game at some bar. He really didn't want to go but thought it would lessen suspicions since he was blowing the guys off on Mondays, Wednesdays, and Fridays and now very possibly this Thursday as well. Stu begged off, but Al said he was up for it, much to Steve's dismay.

They ate downtown after work at Jimmy Wong's on Wabash since they both had a taste for Chinese food. The discussion was the usual talk about the bank, sports, and politics, with some women mixed in. It was rumored that Cremmons hired a new secretary since his current one was retiring, and she was supposed to be a real looker according to a couple of employees who saw her at an interview.

Steve found it difficult and uncomfortable when Al asked him if he was using any more coke and what he thought about all the drug trafficking and busts that had taken place all over the Chicago area and every other place.

"It's like Prohibition," Steve said. "People want something bad enough, but you have a law that runs contrary to that, so they find other ways to get it. Years ago, organized crime supplied all the booze during that time. But they'd have nothing to do with drugs after it ended, contenting themselves with gambling, loan sharking and other sources of revenue. So, when drugs came along big time, there was a void to fill and now the street gangs peddle it and the cartels in Columbia, Mexico and other places are the suppliers and they fill it."

"I'll say they did," responded Al. "I bet the markup on this stuff is huge and some people are making a killing. I'd also bet that they dilute the stuff with flour, powdered sugar, whatever works."

Steve nodded. Best to move back to sports and women, which he did.

He caught the nine thirty-five train and settled into a window seat in a better than half empty train car. He closed his eyes for a bit and then looked out the window, only to see a reflection of himself and someone who was sitting across the aisle from him, staring straight at him. He slowly turned around to see a middle-aged executive type in a jet-black suit and a thin tie pick up his newspaper and turn away. Steve studied the man slowly. He was not dressed as the typical North Shore type. No, the suit looked like it was a cheap off the rack variety and the whole world was wearing wide, somewhat colorful ties these days, except for, except for maybe a cop, fed, narc, who might wear a skinny black one like this guy.

Steve trembled for a minute, looked at his hands, and noticed tremors. He couldn't remember if this guy had sat down after he did and the whole matter could be coincidental. Maybe the guy was just looking out Steve's window, maybe he thought he knew Steve or maybe...

Steve was two stops away and the big question now was whether this guy was going to get off at his stop and follow him or worse. As the conductor announced "Main Street" he gripped his briefcase on the vacant seat next to him and swung it around, so it was on his lap. If this guy stopped him, he had nothing to hide and thank goodness it wasn't tomorrow for the next run. Steve resolved not to look at the man when he got up to get off. It would only increase suspicion.

As the train approached his stop, he got up and fixed his eyes straight ahead to avoid eye contact. He stood in the vestibule of the car, waiting to get off as the train slowed but also waiting to see if the man would come through the door at any moment. Nothing. After departing the station while looking over his shoulder at least three times, he was convinced the entire episode was just happenstance and that his nerves had gotten the best of him. He took some of Becky's old pain pills he still had and soon the drowsiness they produced led to a deep sleep.

Wednesday at work there was an unannounced fire drill which broke up the midafternoon monotony but then an interdepartmental note was on Steve's desk when he returned, stating there was to be a brief meeting on some new federal regulations at four thirty. Hopefully, this wouldn't run late.

There were two speakers at the meeting in one of the bank's several conference rooms. One was Steve's immediate boss, Clay Miller, a fortyish baby-faced banker who looked a lot like Audie Murphy from old western movies, although Miller was definitely much taller and had wire-rim glasses. Miller went first, and he was all business, pointing out the high points of the new regs in literally ten minutes, saying only two were really pertinent.

Then Jerry Leland, an economist from another department, covered the balance of the presentation. His low sing-song voice almost put everyone to sleep as he went over facts and figures behind his large frame Coke-bottle glasses. He acted like he had all day, and everyone was clearly becoming restless as the clock on the conference room wall showed four fifty six. Steve knew he would have to be the first one up if he had any chance of making the train rendezvous, although he hated to do that. It would look really bad. He felt his stomach churn and sweat building behind his shirt collar.

Finally, at five after five, Leland asked if there were any questions and, without giving much time (realizing the time himself) stated, "Good. Thank you all for coming," as if anyone had a choice.

By the time he said "all" Steve was at the door and bolted to the elevator. He rushed to the train, running every fifteen seconds, and walking for twenty seconds in between. He was actually about a minute or two behind his contact for the restroom swap, but could feel his heart pounding as he stood at the urinal to take a leak just a few minutes after the other man arrived.

He boarded the train and collapsed from exhaustion into a window seat. He made it. Someone had even left a Sun Times under the seat in front of him and he thought maybe the day might even end on a high note. He was wrong.

As the train slowed before his Evanston station, he realized he had become too engrossed in an article about the NCAA basketball tournament, and he hadn't been paying attention. Most of the passengers getting off were already in the center vestibule of the railroad car, and the train came to a stop with a loud hiss, signaling that the doors were opening. He quickly got up and trotted for the doors, glancing behind to see two men similarly dressed in black overcoats doing likewise.

Steve made his way through the crowd as they embarked from the train as quickly and deftly as he could, without arousing suspicion. He again glanced over his shoulder to see the two men about twenty feet behind him walking in tandem. His hands became so damp that even in the cold, he felt like he was losing his grip on the briefcase. Once the crowd started to disburse, he broke into a trot to the stairs and bounded down them, but this meant he was a minute or so early for his contact.

He stood at the bottom of the stairway, fearing to look up. People were coming down the stairs, slowly and methodically, not anyone to fear. Another few minutes went by when the short little man with the beard ran up to him to exchange cases.

"You're late," Steve hissed, almost in a whisper.

"Sorry," was all the man could muster as he made the exchange and briskly walked away.

Steve didn't even have a chance to say he was being followed and ask what he should do now. He stood where he was, motionless, with a lump in his throat, still breathing heavily. He looked up the stairs again. Nothing. Silence except for a bus pulling away from its stop around the corner. He started walking home slowly. Had these men been looking for him? If they knew he was on the train, why did they wait? Were they even following him, or was the entire incident just another coincidence?

The biggest question, of course, was should he call Carlos or Manuel and tell them that he thought he was being followed? Then he stopped near his front door, took a few deep breaths and felt like his head had cleared. He decided that if anything happened Friday, imaginary or otherwise, he would call it quits. Period. Meanwhile, he still had to call Angela about tomorrow night.

After mulling it over again over a frozen dinner, he decided to pick up the phone to call Manuel just to talk, but, then he put it down. He thought he was acting like a scared puppy on the one hand, a real wuss because *maybe* he had seen something. Did he want to be perceived that way when he really wasn't sure?

But then he also thought it could be his imagination from the after effects of the coke he was now increasingly using, playing tricks on him. After all, he did think that he saw that old clock radio slide across the nightstand the other night. And another night when he got up to take an aspirin at three a.m. and looked in the mirror, he thought he saw someone behind him. Okay, no more coke till the weekend and let's see what happens on Friday's run. That will be the test.

He called back his folks, who were on the machine, then Riva. Damn her if she wants to fix me up again, but no, she just wanted some information about the bank's hours at the Lincolnwood branch (was he an information service now?). The reality was he knew she was just checking up on him.

Finally, he called Angela. She asked if he could come over, as she wanted to cook him an authentic Mexican meal.

"Some first date," he said, laughing. "I really wanted it to be memorable."

"Who said it won't be?" she replied in a sultry whisper. Now they both laughed. A good sign.

So, it was settled. He would go straight from work to her apartment at Division and State. Thirty-first floor. It faced the lake, naturally.

He was excited, but apprehensive. He had to bring something. Flowers were too personal for a first date. Wine? That would be nice. But what went with Latin food? Sangria? Well, certainly not that kosher Kedem stuff in the fridge. And should he bring a rubber? He thought he still had some from years and years ago, but even if he could find them, they were probably cracked and brittle. Maybe he'd stop for both items at a drug store that carried liquor before he arrived.

The next day he did exactly that, picking up some Trojans and a fairly expensive bottle of tequila, hopping a cab in the middle of rush hour. He didn't know what to expect and thought it was better that way. Did he want something to happen tonight? Emotionally maybe, sexually would be good as well.

After all, didn't sex relieve tension and certainly he was having enough of that? Besides, it had been a long while. The last time was he couldn't remember when. Becky was already very sick, but they both wanted it, needed it. That's how he would describe himself now, tense and *reckless* in just about everything, including tonight.

She was wearing what looked like a satin orange dress which was cut low in the back and her long hair was styled straight but to one side, held in place by what appeared to be a striking ivory comb. She smelled beautiful, like blossoms in a park. He touched her hand in an awkward motion, and she held his arm as she took the bottle from him.

She thanked him for the tequila, and he asked if he could help in any way, insisting that he knew his way around the kitchen even when still married, but especially now.

"Everything's almost ready," she smiled. "Why not just make yourself comfortable on the couch and we'll eat in a few minutes?".

"What about the tequila? I should open that."

"Okay, uno momento, in a minute or so. Why not watch TV? The remote's on the table next to you." He found it and clicked on the news. More about the hostages in Iran. Congressmen were demanding action.

"Oooh!" she suddenly cried out in frustration. Steve thought she had spilled something, but before he could respond, she entered the living room and continued, "Why can't they do something? Estupido! It's been how many days, weeks, months?"

He could see the fire in her eyes as she crossed her arms looking intently at the TV screen. He was startled and could say nothing for what seemed to be an eternity. He had seldom met someone like this. Passion and beauty rolled into one. It even made his wife and just about every other woman he had ever known seem like simple farm girls, except for Lily Stibic, who he met as a freshman in college.

"Too many, that's how many, you're damn right," he finally said, trying to impress her. "They haven't done jack shit, and these poor guys could be tried in some kangaroo court and hung or shot."

She uttered an exasperated sigh and returned to the kitchen. He turned off the TV and followed her, asking where the bottle opener was. Even with all the cooking aromas, her smell lingered with him as he followed her.

Dinner was five or six courses; he couldn't even remember. She put dish after dish in front of him: corn soup, mini fajitas, beef enchiladas, a chili dish, Mexican lettuce wraps, seasoned rice. It just kept coming. His tequila had been a good choice. She said so herself.

The conversation was mostly about food, what they both liked, restaurants where they liked it, and wines and beers. She made him laugh when she told him she had once eaten at a kosher deli as she mispronounced the words for matzah balls and kishka. He finally knew what she was talking about after she described the dishes and that made him laugh even more, then she started laughing. A funny woman is a sexy woman, and it helps if you're gorgeous to boot.

Dessert was a real surprise. Good old hot apple pie, homemade yet. The kind a good old-fashioned American girl would make. It was the perfect end to a perfect meal.

"I gotta admit I'm so glad we didn't eat out," he said as he leaned over the small glass dining room table and looked into those beautiful, dark eyes.

"I knew you would," she smirked. "Rule number one, Angela is always right."

"What's rule number two?"

She leaned across the table and put her finger to his lips. "That's easy. When in doubt, see rule number one." They both burst out laughing.

He helped her clean up, rolling up his sleeves from his white shirt at work. But after a few minutes she said it would be faster if she finished up by herself and motioned for him to sit on the couch where she soon joined him, pushing him to its end as she leaned against him.

"So, Steven Kaufman, tell me more about your life."

"You know most of it. I told you where I grew up, went to school, and got married. And you know I work at a bank and that I'm trying to piece my life back together."

"I can't tell you how much I feel for you to go through something like this so young," she said as she gently stroked his chest.

"Well, I don't need people to feel sorry for me," he replied. "I've had enough of that." That was a hint to her that this can't be a relationship out of pity on her part.

"No, no, I didn't mean it that way. I admire you. Your strength and ability to carry on. Lots of people would have just fallen apart. But despite what you think, you are handling it well. You're moving on whether you think so or not. That takes courage, guts."

It was hard to tell if she leaned forward to kiss him or it was his move, but they kissed long and hard, while he held her head in his hands, and she moved her knee up between his legs. She started to slowly undress him, then herself as she lay on top of him, as he had imagined many times. as long, sculpted fingernails caressed his chest. They kissed again, this time she gently pressed her tongue into his mouth as he reached up to stroke her cheek. Her knee continued to rub against his groin up and down, although it was already hard. He whispered to her if he should put on protection, but she said she had her own protection, and it wasn't necessary.

She was a woman in charge who knew exactly what she wanted, and it was a welcome change for him as he had taken care of a sick wife and made all the decisions about everything for as long as he could remember.

They made love on the couch and when he had come inside her and their bodies separated, she said she wanted more. Sensing he was not up to the task, she grabbed his organ and with her mouth and did things he had only experienced with seasoned sorority girls so many years ago to make it hard again.

So again, they made love, and he came inside her for what was not a long time, although it seemed like forever to him. She got up and kissed him on the forehead as a mother would kiss a child, then went to the bathroom while he fumbled for his handkerchief to wipe himself off. He snapped on the TV remote to catch Ted Koppel on Nightline reporting on the hostage crisis, which meant it was after ten thirty and that they had talked and made love for well over two hours.

When she emerged, she asked him if he wanted to use the bathroom, which he did, noticing what appeared to be a birth control dispenser in the corner of the marble vanity. She hadn't lied.

"You should go," she said when he came out. "It's late."

"Before I do, I want to know something."

"What, like how good you were?"

"No," he laughed a bit. "I know that's important to some guys, but I'm more concerned if we're going to see each other again or if this was a onetime thing."

"You are sweet." She put her arms around his shoulders. "Yes, Steven Kaufman, I would like to see you again."

He kissed her, still smelling that blossom perfume. "Me too." He gathered up his coat and shoved his tie in a pocket, then kissed her again.

She held his hand and walked him to the door and said good night. After she closed the door, she went back to the couch, grabbed a throw pillow, and sobbed.

CHAPTER TWENTY-ONE

Manuel was awakened by the phone next to his bed at seven on a Wednesday morning. It was Carlos. "Can you come by the restaurant at ten?"

"Yeah, sure. What's up?" He normally wouldn't have asked that on the phone, but he was still half asleep. He was very apprehensive lately. Like Steve, only worse. He was sure he had been followed every time he left the house. Plus, every meeting with Carlos lately had meant bad news. Shipments were still being intercepted, people shot at, including Antonio Rendon the other day as he walked out of a Walgreens on Chicago Avenue at Ogden.

Manuel ate a pop tart with some coffee, got dressed and went to a local bank with about fifty thousand dollars in cash. He waited until a certain teller was free, someone who just happened to work for the family who would accept the deposit and not report it as one cash transaction but as separate cash deposits to six different accounts under the names and social security numbers of dead Rendon family relatives.

After the deposit and some small talk with the teller, he headed down to the city. The sky was totally gray and there was light rain. He snapped on the radio to hear a news report about three shootings in the area yesterday. One involved two rival street gangs and the other two were DEA raids where they broke into a store and an apartment, seizing money, guns, and drugs. Two dead, one seriously wounded. The report said one of the raids on the store involved a local clearing house for a drug family run by a Louis Lopez. The Lopez family dealt cocaine and other drugs in the south suburbs. The Rojos brothers had been cousins of the Lopez family, which had broken away to start their own operation, then worked for the Rendons. But there was bad blood between the two families that went back many years. The store raid resulted in the seizure of well over two million dollars' worth of uncut cocaine and a cache of pistols and semiautomatic weapons.

The announcer went on to say that all three incidents involved drugs and that the joint federal, state and local task force that had been formed would continue to crack down on the drug cartels and street gangs. Just what Manuel wanted to hear this morning.

He pulled up to the restaurant, which had no customers at ten a.m., just several employees working to get the place ready for the lunch hour crowd and beyond. Carlos and Antonio were the only other ones in the place, sitting at a booth away from the window. They both looked grim.

"What's going on guys?" asked Manuel. "You sounded like shit on the phone, Carlos."

"Yeah, well, that's what's going on, nada, shit," he retorted. "Five runs intercepted last week. Along Milwaukee Avenue, along Roosevelt Road to Aurora on the west side and into Pilsen on the south. I'm sure we're being hit by the Lopez family and the street gangs with them, and it won't be long until the feds start moving in and taking names. Then somebody flips, wears a wire and then it could be all over. The only shipments that are going through are on the north shore with your banker buddy on the train." Manuel seemed surprised but had heard this before.

"What do you want to do?" Manuel asked, although he knew what Carlos would say. For his own part, he knew what *he* wanted to do. Retire. Get out now. Take some money and open up a restaurant. Have his mother help with the cooking first, then hire someone. Jesus could help. Stop this insanity where you're looking over your shoulder for the rest of your days and your stomach is in knots. But realistically, he knew it was too late to start over.

"We've got to get everyone together and regroup," said Carlos, fairly calm considering the circumstances. "The old channels aren't working. Maybe we recruit some new people, bring in some new blood. I still think we have some leaks from the inside, family or not." He looked sternly at both of them.

Atonio chimed in, always the man of action. "I say we hit back, hard. If it is the Lopez family, let's hit them on their runs, only we be sure not to wound anyone. We leave bodies!"

"The problem with that is you're just drawing more attention to us then," sighed Manuel. "That puts even more heat on us. Then they come back again and hit..."

"Enough!" Carlos slammed his fist on the table. His face, even in the dimly lit room, became as crimson as his shirt. "Tonio's right. We can't let them walk all over us. We'll have a meeting in a few days, some place out in Aurora. The whole family. Everyone down to the pushers and field hombres. We're gonna reorganize everything. But I swear if we're messed with again, we will hit back hard."

The other two nodded and stood up, following Carlos' lead.

"I'll set this up myself," he added. They said nothing and departed.

Manuel was sick to his stomach. He would not dare

challenge Carlos' authority, but what good would it do to reorganize if there were insiders reporting the movements of every shipment? Plus, he wanted out. Then he laughed a little. Fat chance. It would be different if things were running smoothly, and Carlos was in a better frame of mind. Or would it?

As he fumbled for his keys standing by his car, a loud bang shook him and he crouched down beside the car, shaking. Seconds later a truck emerged from an alley down the block and a second backfire resonated from its exposed muffler, which Manuel could now clearly see but which made him feel just slightly better.

CHAPTER TWENTY-TWO

Manuel decided to tell Steve he would call him once a week, from a phone booth somewhere, just to see how he was doing. He was thinking of having Steve go to a phone booth himself to receive the calls, but he didn't want to spook him out. Sometimes Antonio would call. Manuel liked Steve and felt he was like a mentor to him, but didn't want him involved any further than he already was. Steve was informed about all this after that Monday run when he opened his briefcase at home and found a handwritten note.

Steve would tell whoever called in cryptic terms if everything was proceeding as planned. So, if he really did think he was being followed, he'd have to leave a note in the briefcase for them. Then he laughed to himself and wondered if he should mention on the phone, by the way, that he was dating Carlos' sister and talking to her every night.

Steve was starting to enjoy himself. The suit was just the start. His mom had called from Florida and said his Aunt Shirl, who lived in Highland Park north of Evanston, had a ton of leftovers for him from a party she had. It seemed that with all the angst he was going through, his mother's primary concern was that he wasn't eating well.

So, on a Thursday night, he hopped into the Cutlass and headed north. His Aunt Shirl was his mom's older sister, but aside from a few more wrinkles they were almost identical with their bobbed bleached blond hair, blue eyes, and perpetual tans.

The old Cutlass sputtered and lurched forward. He remembered when they got the car, Becky wasn't sure about it until the salesman showed them that when you opened the doors to the coupe, the seats would automatically swing out. She thought that was the coolest thing in the world, and Steve rolled his eyes and nodded. Those swing out seats would ultimately serve them well when she got sick as it was far easier for her to get in and out of the car.

Not only was the car showing its age, but it was a painful memory. He was supposed to be by Shirl at around eight, but he was very early and as he headed west off of Green Bay Road to her new condo building there it was, Lee Klinger Motors. And in the window of the auto dealership, he recognized it immediately, a black Porsche 928S. He gawked at it while he slowed down to put on the brakes and then stopped.

Steve got out of the Cutlass, but his eyes never left the showroom window. In he went and walked straight to the car. He opened the car door and peered inside. That new car smell. He spotted a salesman behind a glass partition who was on the phone. Steve knew everything about the car. This 928S had the bigger 4.7-liter V8 and a four-speed automatic with three hundred horses. The supple black leather interior also had two seats in back and the pop-up headlights, new to the Porsche line.

"The Shark," he heard the salesman behind him say, a tanned guy about five eight with beefy arms and a loosened tie. "Mickey Kaplan," he extended his hand. Steve shook it. "That's what they call this. Beautiful, isn't she? We only get a few of them a month. Want to take her on the Edens (a close by Chicago expressway) for a run?"

"Steve Kaufman. And this is Porsche's first try at a front engine car, huh?"

"Right you are." They talked for a little while and got a car porter to back it out of the show room. The speedometer unbelievably only went up to eighty-five, which they hit in less than five seconds on the highway and when they got back, Steve called Aunt Shirl and said he'd make it another night. It listed at twelve five and Steve knew the base model was almost half that. They settled on an even ten five and when the salesman asked if he needed financing and Steve shook his head and wrote out a check, the salesman's eyes bulged.

He didn't trade the Cutlass in, just asked if the dealership could hold on to it until the weekend when Becky's brother Eric could pick it up for a cousin who was going to Western Michigan University and who Steve knew needed a car and had very little money. They wrapped up the paperwork and Mr. Kaplan thought these shit-eating young bankers seemed to be making a lot of money.

As he drove home, he had a wicked smile on his face. Becky would have never stood for having a German car, but Becky wouldn't have approved of lots of things he was doing or had done lately. And his answer was always the same. She wasn't here. Then again, neither was his conscience as he shook his head.

Still, even though he was concerned about the commuter runs, he loved having enough money to buy anything he wanted. However, that being the case, he had always believed, like the famous mobsters used to do, better to keep a low profile now. When asked, he would explain that the couple had put away some money for a college fund which was no longer needed. This went over well although everyone would want to ride in the car. Al even wanted to borrow it to impress a date and was seriously pissed when Steve flatly said no.

Angela and Steve went out the next few weeks and talked every night. The Como Inn, Don Roth's Blackhawk, George Diamond's, breakfast at Lou Mitchell's, lunch at Manny's and then usually back to her apartment for what was becoming a regular routine, TV on the couch with a line of coke and then into the bedroom.

They would talk about everything, but as time passed, the topic narrowed as to when they were going to tell their respective families that things were getting serious. Steve felt he wouldn't have as big of a problem as Angela would, however, he preferred to still keep dating and remain somewhat clandestine. She felt the opposite, and she prevailed. After all, she said, she had dated other guys for a long time, some non-Hispanic, and Carlos and her family did not care. She had only a limited knowledge of the business, as did most of the girlfriends and wives, and it was better off that way.

Then one evening on the phone, she told Steve she would tell Carlos and her parents and said that if they really loved each other, which they both professed they did, that he too would tell his parents. This was on a Thursday. They were supposed to go to the circus Saturday night and wanted each other to do it by then.

On the phone Saturday afternoon, they asked each other what had transpired. She asked him first. "They understood. They thought it was maybe too soon to have *any* relationship, but they accepted it."

"You're telling me they accepted who I am?" she asked.

"You mean that you're beautiful, yes I think they did."

"Esteban, don't joke about it. Really, did they accept my color, my nationality, my heritage, my religion, you name it?"

"Yes, as far as I can tell. I'm not saying they were thrilled with it, but yeah, they accepted it. What about you?"

She sighed. "My brother was not happy, but it was

easier because he knows you, somewhat. My mother and father acknowledged it, but it's clear they hope it's a short-term thing."

"Well, that's a start, I guess."

"Yes, and it's a good one, at least for now."

When they hung up, he was still as uncertain about things as he had been for weeks. Love, lust, all he knew was that he wanted to be with her all the time. The comparisons with Becky were obvious. He had planned on spending the rest of his life with her, not after a few dates, but after they first met. With Angela it was different. It was more sensual, more physical, more, well, he really couldn't describe it. And the family problems seemed insurmountable. But again, he wanted to be with her, and that was for certain. Before he met her, he had dreamed about her and now she was his. As his grandma used to say, "Be careful what you wish for."

CHAPTER TWENTY-THREE

Things had suddenly and inexplicably become quiet for about two weeks now and Carlos postponed the big meeting but realized the calm would not last, so he finally called the meeting of his entire organization as promised, for eight o'clock on a Sunday evening at the old church in Aurora for what he termed as a "council of war". The church was the organization's main distribution point in the western suburbs, and there were offices and a large meeting room in the basement. It had been a perfect cover for going on two years now.

Everyone was told to come with only two people per car in case whoever the leak was had tipped off the law, or worse, some street gang thugs ready-to-use firearms. Carlos figured he could lose two people, but not four.

Yes, things had been running smoothly but a few days ago two of their top pushers on the near west side had disappeared and Antonio had been shot at again, this time outside of his house, a bullet from a passing car whizzing by his ear. Carlos swore vengeance and came to the meeting with blood in his eye for who he felt was responsible.

It was the Latin Crescents, one of Chicago's oldest and

largest street gangs, which had a loose alliance with the other large drug supplier in town, the hated Lopez family, headed by Louis Lopez and his clan, up in Chicago for two years now, originally from Baja, California. As cocaine filtered down to the masses, Carlos Rendon's family was in direct competition with the gang on their own turf.

Louis Lopez's smaller, south side cartel was reeling lately, having been hit repeatedly by the feds. Maybe that's why things had been quiet for the past two weeks. They had originally proposed a deal with the Rendon cartel, but Carlos would never think of dealing with them, as it would set a terrible precedent for anyone trying to move in on their dominance in the city.

There had been talk of a truce with the Latin Crescents after the first of the year. The gang would be supplied by the Rendons as their product was clearly superior, and higher priced. But they could never agree on a price, and nothing came of it. The gang would stay with Lopez.

Carlos opened the meeting by stating he wanted revenge, and it would be swift. Antonio and another enforcer named Ramon Santos would firebomb a tavern in Logan Square frequented by the Crescents while Manuel would pick two more and do the same at the Lopez's main hangout, another bar and pool hall in Blue Island, way south of the city.

A few people started to question Carlos for a few minutes, including Manuel, stating it would make things worse, but Carlos would hear none of it, finally slamming his fist on the table as they had seen so many times before declaring, "Enough, they've pulled this shit too often! Just finish the job!"

Manuel cringed, knowing better than to argue. In the end, he simply nodded. This was the Delgado scenario all over again. Who he would recruit and how it would all happen was making his head swim.

Now more than ever, he so much wanted to retire and

open up that restaurant. He had saved a lot of money and spotted several locations up near where he lived. Maybe Steve really could help him get a loan for the rest.

His mind wandered for the rest of the meeting, which was fairly brief, but with Carlos telling all his lieutenants that for now everyone had to be patrolling their territories, north, south, and west every single day. He said things needed to be watched more closely, but what he was really thinking was this might flush out the leak, the informer Carlos was convinced existed.

It wasn't just the violence, but the feds were keeping up the heat and it seemed every week a mule carrying drugs in from out of town or a pusher was being arrested and the bail amounts were getting higher and higher.

"We may still have to totally change our distribution system," he concluded. "Let's see how things go and what happens after these hits take place." But he went no further in discussing how this would be done.

Manuel left the meeting with knots in his stomach and a bad headache. To pick out a crew and firebomb the Lopez cartel was something he dreaded. Who could he trust for this? Obviously, someone in the family, but that someone in the family could be the leak. He could call a couple of low-level pushers who seemed loyal and prone to violence. One possibility was Louie Jimenez, a soldier who had purportedly gunned down three men in Sonora some years back simply because they sold him a bad truck. If this were so, he would only need to bring him with no additional help.

He realized if he were caught, his life would be over. Carlos couldn't get him to beat a murder rap. Not now. Not with all the heat from the law on the drug trade. He noticed he was sweating profusely, although his headache seemed to ease.

He started thinking wild thoughts about taking all the money he had and running away where no one could find him.

Of course, he was not at all clear where that would be except to just get in a car and start driving. But what of his family, his brother Jesus, and his mother? He could never see them again. No, he realized he had to call Jimenez.

When he started driving from Aurora, he had wanted to hear the ten o'clock news on the radio when he realized he was almost home and had never turned it on.

CHAPTER TWENTY-FOUR

Steve picked up Angela from her apartment and they caught an early show, Cruising, at the Esquire theater. She had not been hungry earlier, but now she wanted nothing but a big steak. Steve obliged, and they drove to the Golden Ox nearby on Clybourn Street.

They had been seeing each other for over six weeks now and they had become quite intimate. They had slept over in each other's apartments several times and they saw each other during the week as well as the weekends. Steve finally told Burns, Griffin and Stu Fine that he was seeing someone who he met at a bar near his house, never letting on who it was or saying much about her despite being pressed.

On the plus side, the couple found that over time they had much in common, even though their backgrounds were so different. They both liked sports and the Bears, Mexican food (obviously) and a good steak. And they were both Democrats, part of the broad coalition that was breaking apart with Jimmy Carter in office.

Tonight, however, there would be controversy. After they ordered in the restaurant, Steve started to talk about his commuter runs. The service was slow, and he already had two scotches under his belt and felt light-headed and talkative. He went on about how he loved the mule runs, how they scared him at first but now he felt like an old pro and how natural but exciting it all seemed. What a brilliant plan it was he had conceived.

Her eyes flashed. "What do you know of this business?" she started. "It all comes naturally? You think this is a game like when you play pickup basketball with your friends? It's serious. It's life and death for some people. Blood is spilled, people die, sometimes terrible deaths. All for this white powder that makes you feel good for just a little while."

"Angela, I didn't mean it like..."

"No, then what did you mean? Honestly, Esteban, you are still a naïve little gringo. Try growing up around this business and having it be a part of your life for so many years, then see how you like it!" She was practically shouting now and had to catch herself. He realized he had struck a nerve.

"I'm sorry. I won't bring it up again if that's what you want."

"I'm sorry to be so harsh, but yes, that's what I want."

He tried to change the subject, to talk about the movie, even though what he was doing was obvious to both of them. But this suited her just fine for the moment. They held hands during dessert as they hoped things could be like they were, just a guy and a girl out on a date and having fun. The problem was the conversation had brought out differences that were maybe too powerful to overcome.

Steve dropped her off and gave her a peck on the cheek, saying he would call her. She nodded, then hugged him, whispering everything would be okay. He shivered. She got out of the car quickly and he waited for her to enter her building, gazing at that figure in her form fitting coat which he would never get out of his mind, ever, then drove away.

He snapped on the radio just in time to hear the tail end of a news conference with William Webster, head of the FBI, announcing the number of drug trafficking arrests in major cities, including Chicago, where he said the Bureau was having great success.

He had dropped her off somewhat early for a Saturday night and decided to ride around aimlessly in his new car for just a bit before getting on Lake Shore Drive and heading home. He thought about his car and clothes and the money he had socked away in at least half a dozen different banks. What was happiness? What was it supposed to be? The car was great, but he didn't need to buy something so showy. His clothes were expensive, but now that he had them, it was no great shakes.

And Angela was right. The runs were adventurous but perilous and, of course, didn't represent the true nature of drug trafficking, violence, deception and often death. Lives wasted, ruined. He had not been exposed to that and hoped he never would. He was an upper middle class Jewish kid from West Ridge, a doctor's son, a frat boy who went to school downstate and then Northwestern, the Harvard of the Middle West.

But the only reason he was different from his friends and family was because of the untimely death of his wife and now what he did three times a week. He didn't have to be educated to know this couldn't go on indefinitely. A ten-year-old could tell him it would end badly with an arrest, or worse.

Then there was Angela as he stopped at a light and closed his eyes. For the hundredth time, did he really think there was a future with her? What if they went away some place and started over, maybe a small town somewhere, but not too far from family and friends? Yeah, right, Angela in a small town, that would work. He shook his head and headed home. A guy driving a Porsche going in the other direction honked at him as he passed, and he honked back. "I'll miss that," he smiled.

When he got home at about midnight, there was a message on the machine. Angela. She felt bad about the way they parted and wanted to come over.

"It's kind of late, babe," he said. "And is it safe to be out...."

"I'll be fine. And I've got some great blow. I'll bring it."

She was over in half an hour. The coke waited while they made love on the living room couch. Then she spread two thin lines on his small glass coffee table, one for each of them. Parallel lines that would never meet. Parallel lives. Then she said she had an idea while he went into the kitchen for two straws. She took a card and scooped up the coke from one line and put it back in her vial.

"One line?" he asked.

"Yes," she laughed. One parallel line. She told him to stand at one end of the table and she went to the other.

"Go," she said. They sniffed up the cocaine and met in the middle and kissed.

They slept in the bedroom, and he asked if she was happy. She nodded and kissed him gently. Then they fell asleep in each other's arms. In his wife's bed.

CHAPTER TWENTY-FIVE

In the morning she was gone, leaving a note saying she wanted to go to church and that she would call. The phone rang. To Steve's surprise, it was someone he didn't expect.

"Steven, my friend, it's Manny. How are you, amigo?"

"Oh, okay, I guess. A little tired."

"Rough night, eh?"

"Yeah, it was." He wondered if Manny knew who he was seeing. "What's going on?"

"I wanted to ask you a question, and it's kind of up your alley."

"Sure, go ahead."

"Well, you're a banker and I had a question. No, maybe it's a favor to ask you. I'm thinking of opening up a restaurant, actually, buying a place in the north burbs, in Skokie. It's a hot dog place now but I want to turn it into a diner with Mexican type food. I've got half the money to buy the building and all the equipment and change it over, but I need a loan for the rest."

Steve pondered this. He was relieved to know it was about business other than what Manny did for a living. "Wow. That sounds great. What are you talking about to get dollar wise?"

"About eighty thousand total, you know, give or take."

"I think we could work something out to get you approved by one of our guys. I just do loans over a million, but hell, you got a house now right and the loan to value is probably fine if the appraisal and so on check out. I am on the loan committee and could help usher it through. The only thing is I gotta tell you rates are murder."

"This I already know. But you think it can be done? I think I have a good credit history and a long job history with Club Maravel on a good salary."

"I think it would work. Are you retiring or what?" Steve laughed nervously. He hated to use the word.

"Yes, I'm seriously thinking about it. Can't do what I do forever."

"Say, I'll bring home an application unless you want to stop by a branch to pick one up. I'll tell you the form number you need."

"Let me get back to you on that if it's okay with you," he replied.

"Sure. Everything else, okay?"

"It will be," he said, almost in a whisper.

Steve wondered what he meant, but did not press the matter, especially on the phone. "Okay, well, I'll talk to you soon."

"Yes."

Steve pondered the call for a while. Manuel's credit was obviously not the issue. It was where the rest of the money was coming from. What if that money was traced? That could ultimately implicate Steve. And how could he ever explain to the loan committee how he came to know Manuel and recommend his application? He laughed for a second...maybe Russ Cremmons could help him there.

But there were even more serious questions. Why was Manuel contemplating a change in careers? Was something about to happen to cause that change? Manuel had always been straight with him. Wouldn't he tell him if something was coming?

He settled in to watch a basketball game after washing off the table in the living room where the line of coke had been drawn and sniffed. He was finding it harder to get the original buzz he had from the same amount of powder and was using more and more, it seemed, to achieve the same effect.

The phone broke his concentration on the game. It was his father.

"Steven, how are you?" His father didn't talk on the phone. He yelled into it.

"Okay, Dad. How are you and mom?"

"Fine, fine. Listen, Aunt Essie saw you yesterday by the deli near your house, that Zenner's place."

"It's Zengler's dad, not Zenner's." This was the umpteenth time he had corrected him on this.

"Whatever it is. She saw you get into a fancy black sports car. Did you get a new car?"

Steve had to think fast. There was no sense lying about the car, but he obviously needed to lie as to how he paid for it. His great Aunt Essie. That nosey old bag. "Yeah, it's mine. I treated myself to it. I thought I needed a lift with all that's gone on."

"Well, I hope you can afford it and all. What kind of car is it?"

"It's a Porsche and yes, I splurged. We got a bonus at the bank, so I'm really okay on it." This would work except he told the guys at work that he received an inheritance, but when would they see his dad?

"Really? That's German, right?" A new line of attack.

"Yes, but it looks and rides great."

"But your wife would never even ride…"

"Dad, don't start with that. She's gone and even though she wouldn't ride in it, she would want me to be happy." What a crock, he thought to himself.

"I still can't believe you'd do such a thing."

Yeah dad, you told me you were looking at a Mercedes in Lauderdale. "Dad, drop it. If she saw me, why didn't she say hello?" That's sort of changing the subject.

"She was in a car. A friend was driving her to the doctor."

"Oh, that's nice."

"Okay, here, talk to your mother."

Steve's mother proceeded to repeat the story that Aunt Essie had seen him in a fancy car and was it his and how did he get it, ad nauseum.

He slept well that Sunday night, even though he was still concerned about what Manuel had said. Maybe it was time for him to quit as well. He had made some very easy money, but knew he had also been very lucky. Maybe it was time.

CHAPTER TWENTY-SIX

S teve arrived at work about twenty minutes later than usual as the train engineer thought he hit someone crossing the tracks on the way into the city and crew members and police went up and down the tracks but found nothing. When he arrived, one of the other bankers said two men were waiting for him at his desk. To his complete surprise, then shock, they introduced themselves as field agents for the FBI and both pulled out I.D. cards. They asked if there was somewhere that the three of them could talk, and Steve, still in disbelief, directed them to a small conference room in the area.

"What's this about?" his voice quivered.

One of the agents, in his mid-thirties and older than the other, first explained that Steve himself was not under any investigation and that he had nothing to fear, as long as he honestly answered the questions asked of him.

Steve nodded. "Sure, but again, what's this all about?" He was still shaking.

The younger agent pulled out a manila envelope and withdrew two large photos, placing them on the table facing Steve. One was of Carlos Rendon, the other Antonio. They appeared to be prison mugshots. "Do you know these men?" And before Steve could utter a sound, he added, "Think carefully, because we know you were seen with them at Ziggy's bar on Milwaukee Avenue."

Steve had to think quickly and decided an honest approach was best, but maybe not a completely honest one. "Yes, I met with them. They sold me about a hundred dollars' worth of cocaine for my own use. It was a onetime thing. I had never tried it before. I've never seen them again and I'm sorry that I did."

"How did you know to meet them at this place?" asked the senior agent.

"I met them earlier at a club on Rush Street," he replied, feeling the sweat building on the back of his neck. He wanted to at least try to keep Manuel out of this if they didn't know about him.

"You just met them, just like that?" queried the younger agent.

"Well, no, not exactly. I met Carlos in the bathroom at this Rush Street club. He struck up a conversation and found out that I was looking to try some cocaine, and he said he could help. He told me to meet him at Ziggy's and wrote down the address." Steve had to hope that the FBI hadn't staked out Club Maravel, or he was finished, along with Manny.

"What was the name of the club, do you recall? asked the senior agent.

"I think it was called Club Marvel or Maravel, I'm not exactly sure. We were all pretty drunk that night, the guys I was with."

The agents looked at each other and nodded, the junior agent pulling out a note pad and furiously writing this down. It was as if Steve was filling in the piece of some jigsaw puzzle.

"Do you know who Carlos Rendon is?" asked the younger

agent, tapping his picture.

"Not really, except that he deals in drugs."

"He does more than deal," continued the senior agent. "He's one of the largest cocaine dealers in the area and controls a huge drug ring. We've been watching him for months and the only thing I can't figure out is why the hell he would want to deal with you for a hundred dollars, a lousy gram of cocaine?"

"He said he liked me and wanted to help me out. Said I'd never try anything better. It was kind of a pride thing and that was it." There was silence for a moment that seemed to last an eternity.

"Here's our cards," the senior agent finally said as they both again pulled out their wallets in unison. "If he contacts you again, we'd appreciate a phone call."

"Absolutely, but again, it was a onetime thing."

"I hope so, for your sake."

This sort of set the tone for the day. Steve was convinced he would call Manuel, assuming the number was still good, tell him what happened, and tell him further that he wanted out-no more runs, ever.

Steve couldn't concentrate on anything that day. He truly wished he didn't have to make what he considered the final run of his brief career as a drug runner. Why, oh, why did I suggest this? he thought. Was he trying to get back at someone or something? Maybe a God that he no longer prayed to or an entire religion? Well, it didn't matter now because whatever the reason, it was going to be over.

Then he thought of Angela. Again, did he love her or just lust for her? He still didn't know the answer, but was pretty sure that if he called it quits, he would not be able to see her again. He needed a clean break from everything. Could he live with that?

The FBI, holy shit. Yes, they had answered all his questions.

The train ride home was uneventful, except that Steve's visit by the FBI made him look around every few minutes with a knot in his stomach. The switch in the restroom was made at the usual time and the train was crowded, the heat almost unbearable in the car, especially with everyone wearing their heavy winter coats. Even though March was coming to an end, Chicago didn't know it yet. He gave up his seat to an appreciative older woman and went to stand in the vestibule, even though the train still had far to go.

He almost felt a sigh of relief, but the FBI men took away any final thoughts of that. He rubbed their two business cards in his pocket to see if maybe they weren't there-that maybe the whole episode was imagined, a dream.

When his station was called out, he readied himself by the sliding doors, ready to be the first one off the train. The train stopped, and the doors opened with their characteristic hiss and the conductor's familiar cry of "watch your step."

He started to slow up, thinking he might be too early for the final exchange of his short career, then proceeded cautiously and deliberately down the stairway. To his amazement, he saw Manuel coming towards him with a briefcase while behind him two dull thuds from a silencer hit him in the back of the head as he lurched forward towards Steve, the last person he would ever see.

Steve gasped in horror and turned away with his briefcase, hearing several screams, running now in the opposite direction, not caring who noticed and only hoping he wasn't next. Meanwhile, the man who shot Manuel swooped up the briefcase he had been carrying and, as a speeding car careened around the corner and slammed on the brakes, he jumped in.

Steve was running away from the direction of his apartment. He ducked into an alley and realized after he stopped running that he couldn't catch his breath. He crouched over and vomited, believing he was going to suffocate as parts of his lunch were caught in his throat. After a few seconds of spitting and then swallowing several times, he felt that he could breathe, although it was more like panting. He wiped his mouth, picked up the briefcase and started to slowly emerge from the alley, walking slowly north now, further away from the station area.

He planned to reach another street with a viaduct that ran under the tracks and head east under it, ultimately back south towards his apartment. He was still trembling as his hand gripped the briefcase. The back of his neck was soaked under his shirt collar, and his armpits were soaked through his undershirt. He was tempted to ditch the briefcase entirely but was convinced he might reach his own untimely death if he did so.

Upon reaching the apartment, he collapsed on the couch, still in his coat. He washed his face and rinsed out his mouth, staring at himself in the mirror, wondering how things had gone so crazy.

Steve checked his messages. There was just one from Angela asking if he wanted to see "Gilda Live" at the Esquire later in the week. He realized he had to call someone about what happened, but who? It couldn't be the FBI and now Manuel's number was useless, the only one he had to the drug business, when he realized someone would probably contact him.

He didn't have to wait long. Carlos called him about an hour later.

"Steven, you okay?" he asked calmly, almost in a whisper.

"Yeah, but we gotta talk."

"Take it easy. Tomorrow you will meet me at my condo with what you have. Someone will notify you where that is."

"Wait a second. I just saw Manny gunned down in public.

I need to know what's going on, what's happening. And two FBI agents showed up at work today. I can't...."

"Everything will be explained to you. Just sit tight until tomorrow," Carlos interrupted.

Steve was too numb to say anything except a feeble, "okay."

He couldn't eat that night and just took sips from a can of Seven Up. His stomach was now okay, but his head was pounding and once again he went through Becky's old pain killers to find relief. He unplugged the phones and got ready for bed.

But before he got into bed, he did something else he hadn't done since that night at the hospital. He prayed. He was on his knees and started out with the words "modeh ani," meaning I am grateful. Grateful to be alive, grateful to have had a good life despite her death.

He went on, "Oh God, I know these past few months I have denied you even existed in my anger and resentment. That you couldn't possibly be there because if you were, you would not allow such terrible things to happen in the world and to me. You let Becky go after I prayed my heart out and others did as well. I don't think I can forgive you for that. And now I'm asking again for something I probably have no right to ask but I am. Please let me out of this mess that I'm living with. Please give me my life back as if what I have done and these people I know don't exist. Please."

When he was finished, he felt that a wave of cool, fresh air passed over him. He remembered the cantor at his temple describe a feeling of calmness when a person was at peace with themselves: "Adonai Adonai, eil rachum v'chanah," meaning to be in the presence of God. He repeated the words.

These thoughts also helped him to sleep as he wrapped

himself in a comforter and dreamed that he was far away, sitting by a lake in a small town somewhere. Becky's pills had helped again.

The next morning, he felt slightly better. He feared seeing Carlos but also looked at it as a finality. He was going to get out and maybe things would return to the way they once were, even if at the time that didn't seem so great. At least he was comfortable with his old life from the point of not having to live in fear.

He also knew he had to call Angela, if for nothing else than to say goodbye, which he was now resolved to. It was time to find a long-term relationship, another Becky, if possible, if he could get out of this drug life. But he decided not now, not yet.

At work, he wondered what excuse he would make for the two feds who had shown up yesterday. He decided to say that they were investigating one of his customers and that the entire affair was confidential. This had actually happened with another one of the bank officers being questioned a couple of months back and it was all forgotten with the passage of time.

Lunchtime came with another shock. Stu Fine told the boys that Russ Cremmons had disappeared. He hadn't been at work or home for over a week now and no one had heard from him. Steve almost choked on his food when he heard this and feared the worst had happened to Cremmons.

When he returned from lunch, a letter-sized envelope with no outer markings was on his desk. He opened it to find a single piece of paper with an address on Lake Shore Drive and a time: tonight, at eight o'clock p.m. He discreetly put this in his suit pocket and tried to settle in to doing some work in the afternoon.

He then realized that it probably wouldn't be wise to take the commuter train home. What if someone recognized him from yesterday when he got off and called the police on him?

After all, he had the same topcoat on, although he had left the briefcase at home under the bed. He decided to take the Evanston Express, another commuter line run by the Chicago Transit Authority that ran parallel, although a bit west of his regular commuter line.

After grabbing some dinner at a local diner, he came back home and took out the suitcase from the bed. He felt like opening it to guess how much cocaine was inside. He figured the briefcase weighed about ten pounds, but only two pounds when empty. If there were eight pounds of cocaine, that would be ninety-six ounces. At two thousand dollars an ounce (the FBI agent had been way, way off, but he said nothing to him) that came close to two hundred thousand dollars. This is what these men fight and die over. He left it closed and felt that it had not been a great adventure, just a sick experiment that needed to end.

The Porsche travelled smoothly down Lake Shore Drive. Would he keep the car? No, he reasoned. Too much attention, too many questions. More important right now, was he being followed? It was too late to consider that. Just get to Carlos' apartment and try to end this.

He spotted the address on the high rise building and saw there was no parking anywhere on the inner drive, so he gave the car to the valet who was only too happy to take the wheel. Carlos buzzed him up and greeted him at the door in a silk bath robe. He apologized and explained he had just come home and showered. Even though he was only in undershorts and a robe, he had at least three gold chains around his neck that reached down his dark chest.

"Sit down, Steven," he said as he motioned to a couch in the expansive living room. "Can I get you a drink or something to eat?"

"No thanks," he said nervously. "I just ate a little while

ago."

"Fine, fine. I see you have what was supposed to be delivered."

"Did you know Manny showed up for the delivery and someone shot him, and I ran like hell before…"

"I know all about it," Carlos cut him off. "And you're a very lucky young man." Carlos took the briefcase from Steven's side.

"Lucky? How do you figure? I, I just witnessed a murder."

"Lucky because if the exchange took place, you would probably be in police or federal custody, amigo."

"How do you figure?"

"Because for months now, I knew the feds or the cops or whoever had an inside mole on us, and Manny was that mole. We confirmed this not long ago, so if your *friend* had made the exchange instead of your regular contact, chances are you would have both been nabbed. But the difference is you'd still be in jail, and he had to go. We asked Manny to make the exchange, telling him the regular man, Mateo, had been picked up on a minor charge. Manny wasn't leaving his house, and we knew he had plans to leave town. So, we knew where he would be."

"But that's not so," Steven countered. "He wanted to go into the restaurant business. He called me about a loan. I know he hinted at getting out but, I don't know anymore, nothing is what it seems anymore to me."

"Steven, yes, he did more than talk about getting out. However, the only way he could possibly get out cleanly was to flip on all the rest of us. And that's exactly what he did. And that's why we did what we had to do."

Steve swallowed hard because that's exactly what *he* wanted to do, to get out. And if Carlos was saying there was no other way? Still, he had to try and said a brief silent prayer. Here goes.

"Carlos, I made a mistake. I know our arrangement has worked so far, but I know I'm being followed. And the FBI came to my office with pictures of you and your brother. All I said was I met you once and bought some cocaine off you, an ounce. Nothing further. Sooner or later, and I think it'll be sooner, I'm going to get caught. I'm scared. I'm not one of you. I don't do this for a living, and I'd like to get out while I still can."

Carlos looked inside the briefcase, then looked at him long and hard, his eyes seeming to pierce Steve's soul. Then he put the briefcase down. "Your runs have been successful and profitable for us, although Manny let the dope dealers run wild up there, skimming our take, being reckless, letting them take pot shots at each other so that the territory is still a mess. Something else you probably never knew. And then he flips on us. But I can appreciate your situation. You see, what we do is not fun and games but serious business, as I'm sure Angela has told you."

With that, he blushed. "I always realized that," he replied, with his head lowered. "I just didn't think it would get that close to me."

"There is a way we can terminate the relationship where you come out ...whole."

Steven lifted up his head. "How's that?"

"You make a solemn oath, swear on your life to me, because that's what would be at stake, that you will never see or call my sister again."

Steve couldn't believe what he was hearing, like the words weren't real. All sorts of thoughts were swimming in his head, but after a few seconds he nodded and said almost in a murmur, "I understand." He couldn't believe he said this but also couldn't believe that Carlos was asking this of him. Was the relationship that much of a threat to him or what? He dared not to ask.

"Good. Well, that's settled. I have to make a few calls before I go out again."

He rose from the chair and Steve followed his lead. "Go back to your banking, Steven. Stay in your world and leave us to ours."

Carlos walked him to the door and put his arm around his shoulder. "You're an honorable man. You did what you said you would, and I know you will do what I ask". His arm slipped off his shoulder and he reached to shake Steve's hand. "Goodbye, my friend."

"Goodbye Carlos."

He was numb. The news about Manuel and the request about Angela were too much to comprehend at once. But as he got into the elevator, he felt a huge sense of relief and thanked God. His thoughts went back and forth between Manuel and Angela. Manuel was gone. There wasn't much to do about that except had he mentioned Steve to the feds when he flipped? But why would he if he wanted a loan from him? But the FBI coming to his office?

Then there was Angela. Did he love her? Could they ever have been happy together for a long time? He reluctantly answered no to both questions, even if the edict from Carlos had never been issued. But to end it this way without a word. He still wanted her, but finally realized that it was not meant to be.

CHAPTER TWENTY-SEVEN

T he next day, Wednesday, found Steve happy and relieved. No rushing for the train, no excuses to the guys as to where he had to be. He seemed to truly enjoy work, which hadn't been the case for a while. He even listened to Stu, who cornered him to ask if he had ever seen the Black news anchor, Alissa Hightower, on TV. She was going to start a special series on profiling women who wanted to change their lives, which was going to garner big ratings. The first episode concerned a prostitute who was trying to go straight. Stu was, of all things, seeing Ms. Hightower at her apartment on weekends. Steve almost seemed interested.

No one wanted to stay late for drinks, so Steve leisurely strolled to the train, passing the restroom at the station with a slight smile. He stopped for a Tribune and took his time boarding for what seemed like a stress-free ride home.

The message on the answering machine from Angela was a rambling discord. She first stated that she realized their relationship had too many obstacles to overcome and that it inevitably would have to come to an end. But then she praised him and then both of them for trying and tempting fate.

This was followed by sobbing and concluding that love

could still conquer all to the point that it was just trite. She then said she wanted to change her life and leave her family and the drugs behind to get a fresh start. And she often thought that maybe Steven and their relationship was that start.

But she ultimately admitted that the relationship was doomed, if not by Carlos, then by its own nature. So Angela had come full circle. She ended with a tearful goodbye. Steve was tempted to call her back, but thought better of it and put down the receiver. It was over.

Thursday was uneventful, except Steve gave Stu Angela's phone number. Who knows, maybe Alissa Hightower could help her start over. There was a bulletin that was passed around requesting each vice president in the loan department to meet with Clay Miller, the department head, at certain appointed times on Friday. Steve's time was at two o'clock. Miller had arranged these one-on-one meetings for the past several months, so it did not seem unusual to any of the V.P.s.

When Steve arrived at home that evening, he decided to call Barbara from Northwestern, but he got her machine. He asked her to call back. It was time to get on with his life. God had answered his prayer, even though at a price, but he thought it was 'bashert' as his mother would say, that is, it was meant to be. Tomorrow he would place an ad in the Trib to sell the car and start to slowly withdraw the money in the different bank accounts to invest in his own bank where he worked.

Clay Miller started meetings with the vice presidents at one o'clock. His first meeting was with Art Duffin who was junior to Steve but not by much, maybe six or seven months. Duffin came by his desk at about one thirty. His black suit looked rumpled, and his thinning blond hair was unkept and his glasses were crooked. His co-workers would often make fun of his appearance and mannerisms. Art could never make a decision, he was a great pontificator, even about what to eat for lunch. His banking customers would often complain about him because he took so long to get back to them and when he did, he often hadn't decided anything. He stood by Steve's desk.

"Well, that's that," he sighed.

Steve looked up at him. "What do you mean?"

"I mean I've been let go. Two weeks. The cuts are here," he muttered, looking down at the floor sheepishly.

"Oh Art, I'm sorry. I know you've got a kid and all."

"Well, maybe you'll fare better, but from what Clay said it's not looking pretty. Lotta people are gonna be shocked."

"Really." Steve threw his pen down. "Shit, that's comforting to know."

"Yeah, so I'll see ya. I gotta make some calls." He shuffled off while Steve had to catch his breath. He hadn't liked working at the bank lately, except for maybe the last few days, but jobs were tight, and he was scared. What would he do? Something else to worry about now.

He could live off the money he had for a while, but he'd never been unemployed, ever. He worked throughout high school and summers in college, and this was only his second job out of school. Still, there were only a few left in the department with more seniority so maybe he'd make the cut.

Clay Miller was a tall, lanky man, mid-forties with straight blond hair parted to one side and wire-rim glasses. A banker's banker. They had always gotten along but Steve sensed the tension in the room and in Miller's voice as he sat down in the conference room, the same room where he met with the FBI agents.

"Steve, as you know the bank, like most of the economy, has fallen on hard times," he started, folding his hands like a steeple. He went on for about ten minutes. The department was being gutted, there would only be a skeleton staff, and so on. He finally got to the point which by now Steve knew was coming.

"If it were up to me, I'd keep you on, you especially, because I consider us friends as well as colleagues. But it's not my choice. We're going strictly by seniority, and I can only keep three people, all senior to you." Miller was smooth and almost charming, even while delivering bad news.

Miller would arrange for three weeks' pay and a 'bonus' as they would term it in lieu of calling it "severance pay." He asked Steve if that seemed fair and Steve said yes, although his pension wasn't fully vested, which Miller acknowledged and said he'd get the bonus "kicked up" and would let him know the final figure by the end of the day. Miller shook hands with him saying the only good thing about this was maybe Steve needed a rest after all he'd been through lately. If he only knew.

When you're let go from a job but given time to stay on no one ever expects you to do anything in the interim and Steve was no exception. But Steve planned on that Friday being his last day at the bank. He made some notes on a few loan files, organized his files so someone else could follow them, took the numbers of a few customers he would call from home and waited for the train. Al, Stu, Jack, even his new secretary who wasn't in today, the hell with them. Goodbyes were not necessarily his thing lately.

Miller's secretary came by with a note in an envelope which just had a figure on it and Steve smiled briefly, he had been good to his word. He walked out and took an early train.

That night he called his parents. It was a painful call to make. He really didn't want to talk to anybody. His father was upset but as usual, his mother was upbeat. "You'll find something," she said. "I believe when one door closes another opens." She had used that hackneyed phrase for years, as her mother did before her.

Barbara also called him back. He asked how she was doing

and explained the situation. She thought it was a shame and how he had sounded so cheerful when he called and left a message. They talked for some time. He didn't feel like setting up a date but did say he'd call back, again reminding her that he told her way-back that he would call her again and that he was good to his word.

The weekend found him often in a trance-like state. He still couldn't believe all that had happened in one week: Manuel's death, getting out of the drug trade, losing Angela, and finally being laid off. Saturday he was up early to go to the different banks and clean out the accounts. He obviously no longer wanted to invest in accounts where he had worked so he simply had cashiers or bank checks made out to himself and put them in his safe deposit box he had at the last bank.

He hit the gym in the afternoon, made himself dinner, which he was becoming quite adept at, watched TV and did a little over one milligram of coke. Then, before putting the bag back in the closet behind the coats, he stared at it. The bag held less than an ounce now. "You know what, fuck you!" He crumpled it up and flushed it down the toilet.

The next morning, he awoke to the ringing of the phone at about nine thirty.

"Hello, Steve?" a voice asked.

"Yeah, who is it?" he mumbled.

"It's your cousin Roy down in Carrol, Illinois," the voice said in an upbeat rhyme.

"Hey Roy, how are you?" Steve rasped as he cleared his throat.

"Fine Steve, just fine. I called to see how you are, but I think I know since I just hung up with your mom."

"Oh really? Well, I'm sure you talked to her longer than I

usually do," Steve said with a wry smile.

Roy chuckled. "How's it been, are you okay alone?"

"Yeah, I manage. I was a bit of a recluse for a while, but I've been going out, doing things."

"Good. So, listen," Roy continued. "We've got a small bank down here in Carrol and the senior vice president just retired, going to Sun City in Arizona. I know they're looking for someone and I know the president. You think you might be interested? You'd have to move down here cause it would be a hell of a commute but if nothing's holding you up there, it would be great."

Steve scratched his head rapidly. "Gee, I guess I could come down, scope it out and see what there is."

"Aww, you'd love it down here. Everyone's friendly. People leave their doors unlocked, the cost of living is cheaper, it's just a slower pace."

"What about you being Jewish and all? I never figured out how you got away with that down there."

"Hey, they don't care if your Jewish, Muslim, Hindu or whatever. Everybody gets along, unless you're a real estate developer. They don't like them much."

"I've had them for customers and for most of them I'd agree with that." They both laughed at that. "Well okay Roy, how do we pursue this?" Steve seemed genuinely interested and had nothing else to follow up on.

"Leave it to me. I'll have the bank president give you a call. His name is Wilfred Atwater. Can he call you at home day or evening?"

"Sure, at this number. I'm not going into work anymore."

"Good deal. Home is better anyway. He's a real folksy type,

like a lot of people are in town. You'll like him."

"Okay, Roy. How's your business and your social life?"

"Good on both counts. Everyone wants stained glass, especially up your way. And I date, nothing serious yet."

Steve had to take a leak. "Well, you take care now. When I come down there you can show me around."

"You got it. I'll talk to you soon."

Steve sat on the edge of the bed and thought for a moment. This could be something, *if* he could adapt. A small bank. It would mean more responsibilities for sure and probably less pay. But he was interested. Maybe his mother's words would ring true.

CHAPTER TWENTY-EIGHT

Monday morning Steve took his car to get washed, did some shopping and just drove around. He was going to miss his car radio with that great stereo sound as he listened to I Love Rock and Roll by Joan Jett and Once in a Lifetime by the Talking Heads.

At about four thirty he was about to jump in the shower when the phone rang. "Steve? This is Wilfred Atwater from the Midland State Bank down in Carrol, Illinois," a booming voice said through the phone. "Is this an okay time to talk?"

"Yes, it's fine," Steve replied.

"Well, I've been talking to Roy Fine, and he says we might have some mutual interests. We've got a guy retiring down here and hear you might want a job."

"That's right. We've had a series of layoffs up here at our bank, Columbia National, including me. Last Friday was my last day."

"So, we've got this opening, but I don't know if you'd be a good fit. You see this fella who's retiring did *all* our loans, everything from cars to homes to credit lines. And I understand you dealt primarily with real estate."

"Yes, that's what I did." Steve didn't want to elaborate just yet, to say he could probably jump right in and learn whatever it was this guy did.

"I guess it isn't your fault or anything. It's just that your high falutin' banks are so compartmentalized and all, but then again, I suppose it's not anything someone bright enough couldn't pick up. And the pace would be such that there'd be a lot of learning time. Hell, Howard, that's the fella's name, took his time to learn everything, probably years when you think about it."

Steve felt very comfortable hearing this. He decided to make the next move. "Yes, that may be the case. I think I'm a quick learner. I'd like to meet you and see the bank and the town."

Atwater was waiting for that. "Splendid. When would you like to come down?"

"How's Wednesday?" Steve said. He didn't want to seem too anxious.

"Great. How's ten o'clock? I'll give you directions."

"Oh, that's okay. I'll get them from Roy as I'm obviously seeing him too."

"Fine, fine." Atwater seemed genuinely excited. "That's great. See you then, Steve."

Steve called Roy who described Atwater as an older man in his sixties who knew everyone in Carrol and was very likable. The day would work out well since on Tuesday someone was coming by mid-afternoon to look at the car. Roy gave him directions and wanted him to meet with him at nine o'clock for breakfast at some diner.

Atwater hadn't said anything directly about moving down to Carrol, but Steve decided to broach the subject with Roy who thought he'd have to be crazy to commute from Evanston, it would be at least two and a half hours each way.

"You'd like living here," he said. "It would be a fresh start."

Steve agreed that it would be, however, it would make for a hell of a transition.

He fumbled through a file in the bedroom closet and found his most recent resume which he had printed up about six months ago when rumors were first rampant about layoffs at the bank. It wasn't very lengthy, the bank and a prior one being his only jobs after college. He inserted what he additionally did at Columbia National on a word processor which stored his old resume. Maybe he should have more printed but decided to see what happened Wednesday. He found a manila folder to put it in and take with for his meeting with Atwater.

Tuesday an ex professional minor league athlete, now a realtor, came by to look at the Porsche. Steve let him take it for a spin and he said he would call later in the week if he wanted it. Steve was not happy about driving the car to a small downstate town with four thousand people as he definitely thought this would create the wrong impression, however, he was left with no choice.

The next day he got up early and left home around six fifteen for the long drive to Carrol. He followed Interstate 55 south to State Route 113 for a few miles when he came to the green and white sign announcing "Carrol, Population 4,565." Route 113 was also the main street where he quickly saw a one-story brick building at a corner with the name Annie's Diner on a black and white sign above a doorway. The streets seemed deserted except for a stock boy putting items out in front of the local Ace Hardware store.

Steve entered the crowded diner to the smell of sausage, syrup and coffee, along with the clatter of dishes and various conversations. Roy waived to him from one of the yellow padded booths. A girl was sitting next to him.

"Hey Steve, you found it," Roy beamed. He wore a wool shirt with his t-shirt showing at the neck. Roy was in his early forties with black hair that was combed down to cover his forehead and a beard over a ruddy complexion. His hands were rough when Steve shook them, and he immediately remembered that Roy worked with his hands.

"Your directions were good," Steve said. "And I made better time than I thought," he said as he looked at the clock on the wall behind the counter where several diners were eating, which read eight fifty.

"Steve, this is Alice, she works for me at the shop." Alice had a small round face hidden by large glasses and brown hair that fell on her shoulders. She appeared to be maybe in her late twenties. They both said hello at the same time and laughed about it.

"You eat here every day?" Steve asked.

"No, maybe twice a week. I make breakfast the other days. I've got a house around the corner and Alice lives in an apartment above the store."

"So, you both walk to work. Gee, I can't remember the last time I knew somebody who did that," Steve laughed as did the other two.

"I bet you can't," said Roy. "It's all part of good, clean country living."

Steve ordered breakfast from a small plastic menu sitting in a metal holder as the other two had already ordered. The food was great, and the conversation matched it. They told him all about the town and tried to convince him that they were not in isolation on an island somewhere, that they sometimes went up to Chicago and how it wasn't a big deal. The only time Steve felt a bit uncomfortable was when Alice asked about his car, as she could see it through the window, how nice it looked and if he had it long. Steve sluffed it off saying he was getting rid of it soon because the insurance was out of sight.

They talked about the job and Atwater. How nice he was and that he should feel at ease when talking to him, just be yourself. Roy asked about the family and again apologized for not being at the funeral. Steve again assured him it was all right and that the note he had sent was one he would always remember.

Soon it was almost ten, and the diner had pretty much cleared out. Steve could see people walking along the street now and thought that maybe ten o'clock was some sort of magical time when people started working. Roy asked him to stop by the shop after his interview, explaining that the bank was one block down on the other side of the street and that his shop was another two doors down. Roy picked up the check and wished Steve luck, as did Alice.

Midland State Bank was in an old, stately gray building with Gothic columns in the front, like something you might find in any small town where usually the bank and the courthouse are the prominent structures. As Steve opened one of the huge glass and wood double doors, he noticed the old wooden floors, that creaked as he walked. There were two tellers at their stations, one side with waist high writing tables and some worn, overstuffed chairs on the other. Steve saw no one else save for the tellers. He approached the nearest one who was all of eighteen and smiled at him.

"Hi, I'm looking for Mr. Atwater."

"Just go right through the gate," she smiled, as she pointed to two waist high wooden gates flanked by old oak railings on each side which separated the first part of the bank from what appeared to be offices in the back.

"Thanks," he nodded. Steve felt he had been in the bank

before, somewhere else, maybe in a dream or in a place he couldn't remember. Beyond the gate he saw a few desks and several offices that had floor to ceiling glass on the fronts and sides. Only one was occupied. Two women were at their desks, one pecking at a typewriter, the other on the phone. Steve went over to the woman on the phone as he reasoned she was at the desk closest to the occupied office. She was an Asian woman, middle-aged, whose hair was arranged on her head so that she appeared to be a Geisha girl from a movie. He politely waited for her to finish her call when he asked, "I'm here to see Mr. Atwater. I have a ten o'clock appointment."

She smiled and nodded after which she proceeded to get up and walk back to the office, peering her head in for a moment to announce him. She came back, still smiling, "He'll be right with you," she said in perfect English without the slightest trace of an accent.

Wilfred Atwater was a large man with a huge belly and a reddish face disguised by a gray, bushy moustache. He had only tufts of white hair that went in no particular direction and wore red suspenders that seemed like they were stretched to the limit and a red tie which would have been a proper length except for his girth.

"Steve, Steve, it's good of you to make the trip."

Well of course I'm going to make the trip, Steve thought, it's a job interview.

"Thank you. It wasn't that difficult to find, and I made good time."

"Come on into my office, oh hell, let's go into the conference room, my office is a damn mess with papers on the chairs and all." He motioned for Steve to follow him. The conference room was a small room with an old carved wooden table covered by a glass top and surrounded by eight rickety-looking wooden chairs. Steve thought if Atwater sat in one it would surely collapse.

"Let me tell you about our little bank here," Atwater began, folding his hands on the table. And he proceeded to tell him how his family started it at the turn of the century when the town was founded and how his father and grandfather had been the presidents. Everyone in town used the bank and how they finally installed one of those new-fangled ATM machines after much resistance. He then told Steve that he was replacing someone retiring due to illness and what his functions were, elaborating a bit, but not much more, than he said on the phone.

Atwater asked Steve if he had any questions and Steve simply asked what the salary was and if there were any benefits. Atwater replied with a figure that was surprisingly not that much less than what Steve was making, and that health insurance and a matching retirement fund were in the package. Steve was impressed as he believed in a small town there would be a huge salary differential and few benefits. But Atwater had said this is a very senior position in the bank as he explained there was only the controller and Atwater senior to him and one junior officer below him.

Atwater wanted to wrap things up. "Well now I've got two questions for you. One is, are you interested? And two would be, when could you start?"

Steve was puzzled. The second questioned sort of presupposed the first. "Yes, I'm very interested and in about two weeks."

"Good," Atwater said, slapping his knee and rising up, Steve following suit. "Of course," he pondered for a second, "I've got to run this by the board. But that shouldn't take but a day or two, then I'll call you right away if that's okay. At home, right?"

"Sure," Steve said. This sort of took him by surprise. "As soon as you know."

Atwater then proceeded to walk him around the bank, explaining a few things. The second floor was simply for record storage and the controller and other officer weren't in, so it was a quick tour. He showed him the lunchroom and where the fax machine was and walked him to the front door. They shook hands and parted. Steve looked at his watch, it was just ten twenty. He realized he never even gave Atwater his resume.

He walked down to Roy's glass shop and rapped on the door. Roy came outside, lifting his safety glasses to the top of his head. "It smells in there from a stain I'm using, so how'd it go?"

"I think it went well. He said he'd let me know in a day or two, that he had to run it by the bank board."

Roy laughed at this. He laughed hard.

"What's so funny?" Steve questioned.

"The bank board is three people," he replied, still laughing. "Atwater, his wife and the mayor of the town who does whatever Atwater wants."

"Unbelievable," was all Steve could say. Life in a small town.

"You'll need a place to stay," Roy turned serious. "Until you get settled, you can stay in the second apartment over the store for however long you need. Alice has the other one. Come on, I'll show it to you."

They went upstairs and walked through a cozy little apartment which had two bedrooms and a bath, the second bedroom being about the size of a walk-in closet in some homes. But it would do. It was remarkably clean, Roy explaining that an old widow who moved to Texas to be with her sister was its last occupant. The cousins hugged and parted, Steve promising to call when he heard from Atwater.

The next morning Steve received a call from the athlete

who wanted to buy the car if Steve would lower the price by five hundred dollars. Steve expected this. "Done," he proclaimed and asked if he could hold off until the weekend to give him time to shop around for something else to which the man readily agreed.

That same night Steve picked out a blue Chevy Malibu at Z Frank Chevrolet on Western Avenue and went home late to eat leftovers while watching the ten o'clock news. The lead story was about how two alleged drug dealers died in a gun battle with Chicago police and DEA agents on the near west side. They were described as brothers, Carlos and Antonio Rendon. Steve almost choked on his lasagna. He turned up the volume and shivered.

The newscaster continued. Not only were the brothers killed in the shoot-out but earlier in the day Carlos' apartment had been raided by police, where they uncovered over forty-four pounds of cocaine with a street value of well over one million dollars, along with three hundred thousand dollars in cash and several semi-automatic weapons and handguns.

Steve shook his head in disbelief. He was just talking to Carlos a week ago in that very same apartment. He quivered for a second and couldn't hold his fork. Was he finally, really safe? Had others been nabbed? Would they talk and mention his name? The report went on to say that authorities were closing in on what was left of the ring, the Rendon Cartel as they called it.

And what about Angela? Was she an accessory? Was she safe? What if they picked her up and squeezed her for names and his came up? He hadn't thought about that, but it was possible. He started to pick up the phone but then slammed it down. He bit his lip hard. My life with her is over. Don't revisit it. Stay away. Even with some Jack and Becky's pills he didn't sleep well that night.

Friday morning Atwater called right at ten o'clock. "Steve, I think I have good news," he started. "We'd like you to join the

Midland family if it's all right with you."

"I'd be happy to, Mr. Atwater," Steve said smiling as he thought about the board of directors meeting.

"Call me Will. That's just fine Steve, just fine. You figure you can be down in a couple weeks, get settled and everything?"

"Yes, I'll call my cousin right away. Shouldn't be a problem."

"Good. Well, we'll talk again before you get down here. Have a good weekend."

"You as well."

About ten minutes later Al called him, from home. After yelling at Steve for not saying goodbye and Steve explaining it wasn't anything personal and that he just wanted to get out as fast as possible, Al went on to tell him that he and Jack had since received their notices and Stu was told he would be handling the work of one other attorney who was let go in the law department. When Al asked him what he was going to do Steve said he didn't know, maybe move away. For a number of reasons, he didn't want to say that he'd gotten a new job.

Still, he felt like celebrating with someone. Out of desperation and the lateness of the day he finally called his Aunt Edith and asked if they wanted to meet him for dinner, his treat.

"It's Friday Steven, and I made a roast," she said. "You come here."

And so he did. He talked about his new job, his new life and politics with Edith and Bernie. And the evening didn't seem so bad after all.

CHAPTER TWENTY-NINE

S teve went down to Carrol several times over the next two weeks, staying with Roy but trying to get the apartment ready at the same time. Alice helped pick out curtains and some furniture, which, believe it or not, the Ace hardware store carried. Steve met many of the townsfolk at Roy's house, they had all heard about the new banker in town.

One night, while eating dinner at Roy's house, Alissa Hightower from channel 7 ABC News in Chicago did a report on women trying to change their lives. Steve suddenly remembered giving Stu Angela's number. There was Angela, being interviewed. She would stop every so often and sob softly, telling her family history and how ABC, through Ms. Hightower, was helping her complete her GED and then her beauty school education so she could go on to run her own beauty shop. Steve could only smile and mutter, with a few tears himself, "Good for you, Angela, good for you."

He went out to sit on the porch swing. The house overlooked a small lake. Even though it was late March, it was a balmy fifty plus degrees outside. Life was good. He was staring at the sky. There were so many stars that you could see out here, unlike in the city with the haze and glare from all the lights.

Alice yelled from inside if he wanted any tea and he replied yes. A little while later he felt a tap on his shoulder. The tapping continued, but it was more forceful now and he turned around.

"Mr. Kaufman," the nurse said. "Wake up Mr. Kaufman, you've been out quite a long time."

Steve rubbed his eyes and turned around in the worn, vinyl chair. "Huh?" was all he could manage.

"The doctor is coming in momentarily. He has the latest test results from a few hours ago. You poor thing, you slept here the whole night. She's really doing better. She was up half an hour ago for a few minutes and then went back to sleep, but it was so short we all didn't have a chance to wake you."

Steve's head was still cloudy. The hospital room had a second nurse who was apparently taking a woman's vital signs. Two doctors entered the room and asked the nurse leaning over her bed what the results were.

"Good, very good," was what Steve heard.

"Mr. Kaufman how are you?" one doctor said looking at him three inches from his face with his almond eyes. It was Dr. Lee who Steve finally recognized as Becky's primary oncologist. "You're quite a trooper staying here all night. And so is that wife of yours. It's like a miracle or something but her lungs are all clear, not even the tiniest spot. Yessir, complete remission is what it looks like for now. All Steve could do was smile and nod.

And then she awoke. They all asked her how she felt and if they could get her anything. Steve got up and leaned over her bed. It was then that she turned her head towards him and smiled. "A dog," she said. "I want to get a dog."

And through the tears he laughed and nodded okay.

THE END

The Steve Kaufman Series

Book 1: August of 68'

Book 2: The Parallel Line

Book 3: Ready Positions

West Ridge Publishing Co.

Elliot Lei is a real estate executive with two prior nonfiction books. This is his second work of fiction. He lives in suburban Chicago and commutes Dallas.

You can connect with Elliet Lei below:

My email is: elliotlei063@gmail.com.

My X (formerly Twitter) account is: Elliotlei7